Institutional Factors and Students Retention

"A Study of How Institutional Factors are Related to Students in Schools and Colleges"

DR. RAFAEL ALVERIO, PH.D.

iUniverse, Inc.
New York   Bloomington

iUniverse books may be ordered through booksellers or by contacting:

iUniverse
1663 Liberty Drive
Bloomington, IN 47403
www.iuniverse.com
1-800-Authors (1-800-288-4677)

Because of the dynamic nature of the Internet, any Web addresses or links contained in this book may have changed since publication and may no longer be valid. The views expressed in this work are solely those of the author and do not necessarily reflect the views of the publisher, and the publisher hereby disclaims any responsibility for them.

ISBN: 978-1-4401-9945-5 (sc)
ISBN: 978-1-4401-9946-2 (ebook)

Printed in the United States of America

iUniverse rev. date: 01/22/2010

ABSTRACT

The purpose of this study was to determine the characteristics of the students who decided to abandon the Airway Science Program at Inter American University of Puerto Rico and the factors which influenced their decision to do so. Two hypotheses were stated: There exists a significant relationship between satisfaction with the institutional factors and the students' attrition, and there exists a significant relationship between the students' educational goals and decision to abandon the Airway Science Program at Inter American University.

The population in this study was composed of 434 students who decided to abandon the Airway Science Program at Inter American University. The sample scrutinized consisted of 152 subjects (35%). The research instrument used in this study was a questionnaire. The questionnaire was analyzed by computing frequencies and percentages of responses for each item and by computing a cross-tabulation between certain items, where appropriate.

Some findings demonstrated that the number of semesters that the students attended the Airway Science Program at Inter American University before dropping out, was correlated with the interval scale independent variables in the study.

Major conclusions arrived at are: 1) There is a significant relationship between the satisfaction with the university services and the number of semesters that students attend the Airway

Science Program at Inter American University before dropping out and 2) there are significant differences between the evaluation of institutional factors and the number of semesters that the students remain enrolled.

In view of the results obtained from this study it is recommended that a plan of action be designed which focuses on all personal and institutional factors that affect student retention and fosters their achievement of educational goals.

THE NATURE OF SCHOLARLY RESEARCH
INTRODUCTION

Research and evaluation studies fall according to how well they measure up to established scientific standards of excellence.

The most effective insurance against errors is sound and thorough planning which foresees problems and makes acceptable allowances where unavoidable difficulties exist. A study should anticipate its own limitations and choose the most appropriate and powerful solution to a given problem.

Research is oriented toward the development of theories and its most familiar paradigm in the experimental method, in which hypotheses are logically derived from theory and put to a test under controlled conditions. Research has its origin in science. Evaluation has come the way of technology rather than science. Its emphasis is on product delivery or mission accomplishment and not on theory building. Its essence is to provide feedback leading to a successful outcome defined in practical, concrete terms. The advent of the computer altered the informal process to a more formal version. Computers store and process information rapidly and economically, analyzing large volumes of data with complex statistical programs.

There are three steps in a systems approach: (1) setting objectives; (2) designing the means to achieve these objectives; and (3) constructing a feedback mechanism to determine progress toward, and attainment of, the objectives. First, it is determined what the system must accomplish (output); second, all the intermediate steps to accomplish this outcome must be programmed (processing); and thirdly, all the necessary ingredients to be fed into the system must be determined (input).

RESEARCH AND EVALUATION

Planning research studies:

Research investigations require careful planning similar to that found in evaluation studies. Central to a research investigation is a clear-cut statement of the research problem. Attention is given to (a) steps to be taken in analyzing a problem situation and in formulating the problem statement, (b) citation of the advantages of completing the pilot study, (c) an enumeration of common mistakes often made by graduate students in research endeavors, and (d) planning stages to be undertaken by a computer in processing and analyzing data.

Steps in preparing a research investigation are:

Problem analysis:

- Select a problem that engages your attention and begs for a solution.

- Accumulate the facts that might be related to the problem.

- Settle by observation whether the facts are relevant.

- Trace any relationships between facts that might reveal the key to the difficulty.

- Propose various explanations (hypothesis) for the cause of the difficulty.

- Ascertain through observation and analysis whether they are relevant to the problem.

- Trace relationships between explanations that may give an insight into the problem solution.

- Trace relationships between facts and explanations.

- Question assumptions underlying the analysis of the problem.

<u>Ten steps in planning good research</u>

1. What has caught the researcher's interest or has raised a question in his mind.

2. Could it be fitted into a conceptual framework that gives a structured point-of-view? Can the researcher begin from a position of logical concepts, relationships, and expectations based on current thinking in this area? Can the researcher build a conceptual framework into which his ideas can be placed, giving definition, orientation, and direction to his thinking?

3. What does the researcher plan to investigate? What are the general goals of the study? Define the problem.

4. Questions with reasonable answers expected at the end of the research study.

5. The specific objectives at which the research is aimed should be spelled out by the researcher.

6. The researcher should state his subjects, how they should be selected, the conditions under which the data will be collected, treatment variables to be manipulated, what measuring instruments or data-gathering techniques will be used, and how the data will be analyzed and interpreted.

7. What assumptions has the researcher made about the nature of the behavior he is investigating, about the conditions under which the behavior occurs, about his methods and measurements, or about his relationship of the study to other persons and situations?

8. What are the limitations surrounding the researcher's study and within which conclusions must he be confined? What limitations exist in his methods or approach sampling restrictions, uncontrolled variables, faulty instrumentation, and other compromises to internal and external validity?

9. How has the researcher arbitrarily narrowed the scope of his study? Did he focus only on selected aspects of the problem, certain areas of interest, a limited range opf subjects, and level of sophistication involved?

10. The researcher lists and defines the principal terms he will use, particularly where terms have different meanings to different people. Emphasis should be place on operational or behavioral definitions.

Guide to research designs, methods, and strategies

The next step after the research study has been formulated is to construct the research design. The researcher should know what approach to the problem will be taken and methods to be used, and most effective strategies. Design decisions depand on the purposes of the study, the nature of the problem, and the alternatives appropriate for its investigation. Once the purposes have been specified, delimited target area. The nature of the problem then plays the major role in determining what approaches are suitable. Design alternatives can be organized into nine functional categories based on these differing problem characteristics:

Historical, Descriptive, Developmental, Case or Field, Correlational, Causal-comparative, True experimental, Quasi-experimental, and Action.

The **historical** method is to reconstruct the past objectively and accurately, often in relation to the tenability of an hypothesis. Example: A study reconstructing practices in the teaching of spelling in the United States during the past fifty years; or tracing the history of civil rights in the United States education since the civil.

The **descriptive** methods to describe systematically a situation or area of interest factually and accurately. Example: Population census studies, public opinion surveys, fact-finding surveys, status studies, task analysis studies, questionnaire and interview studies, observation studies, job descriptions, surveys of the literature, documentary analyses, anecdotal records, critical incident reports, test score analyses, and normative data.

The **developmental** method is to investigate patterns and sequences of growth and/or change as a function of time. Example: A longitudinal growth study following an initial sample of 200 children from six months of age to adulthood; a cross-sectional growth study investigating changing patterns of intelligence by sampling groups of children at ten different age levels; a trend study projecting the future growth and educational needs of a community from past trends and recent building estimates.

The **case and field** method is to study intensively the background, current status, and environmental interactions of a given social unit: an individual, group institution, or community. Example: The case history of a child with an above average IQ but with severe learning disabilities; and intensive study of a group of teenage youngsters on probation for drug abuse; an intensive study of a typical suburban community in the Midwest in terms of its socio-economic characteristics.

The **correlational** is to investigate the extent to which variations in one factor correspond with variations in one or more other factors base on correlation coefficients. Example: To investigate relationships between reading achievement scores and one or more other variables of interest; a factor-analytic study of several intelligence tests; a study to predict success in college based on intercorrelation patterns between college grades and selected high school variables.

The **causal-comparative** method is to investigate possible cause-and-effect relationships by observing some existing consequence and searching back through the data for plausible casual factors. Example: To identify factors related to the "drop-out" problem in a particular high school using data from records over the past ten years; to investigate similarities and differences between such groups as smokers and nonsmokers, readers and nonreaders, or delinquents and nondelinquents, using data on file.

Contents

List of Tables

List of Figures

CHAPTER I
INTRODUCTION

A major problem among college administration is the declining enrollment of students. "Where have the students gone?" an article in <u>Change</u> (1983) warns of a 26% decline by 1994. The consequences of students leaving higher education are of great concern, both for the individuals who leave and for their institutions. For individuals, the occupational, monetary, and other societal rewards of higher education are in large merit conditional on earning a college degree. It is commonly recognized that a college degree, specially a four year degree, is an important certificate of occupational entry to more prestigious positions in industry and society.

For the institutions of higher education the consequences of high rates of student departure are very important to institutional planners. The experience of student departures and the resulting low enrollments vary among institutions. While some institutions continue to experience gains in enrollments, many have undergone dramatic declines. The competition for students has intensified and institutions have become more skilled in using new marketing and recruitment techniques. It appears that schools have come to view the attrition of students as a necessary course of action to insure the health and survival of the institution.

Students' outcome appear to be the product of a series of sociopsychological interactions between the characteristics students bring with them to college and their institutional experiences while enrolled (Tinto, 1975). Tinto indicated that student departure from institutions can be viewed as a result of a longitudinal process of interactions between an individual, and members of the academic and social systems of the institution. He further states that positive or integrative experiences reinforce student persistence and commitment both to the goal of college degree completion and to the institution in which the person finds him/herself. Negative experiences serve to weaken intentions and commitments to the institution, and thereby increase the likelihood of their leaving school.

Every university institution has a mission and objective. The mission of a university is to give a wide and relevant education in the students' appropriate discipline. It should succeed in graduating the student with maximum skill in his field of study. To demonstrate an appropriate level of competency and to reach these goals, it should offer, besides the academic experiences a series of services and opportunities that meet the needs of the student. To reach maximum development in the multiple disciplines is the responsibility of the University's education.

When a university institution does not conform with its objectives it fails in its mission. Therefore, it does not promote an integral formation, inducing the desertion of its students.

In agreement with Tinto (1987), a student does not remain in the institution if she/he does not meet the objectives established by the institution. If a student transferred to another institution to finish her/his academic career, he/she is not a drop-out. If that student transferred to another institution to continue her/his studies in another concentration, he/she is a drop-out.

Background

InterAmerican University of Puerto Rico, is a private, non-sectarian, non-profit institution, founded in 1912 as a private secondary school at San German in the Southwestern corner of Puerto Rico. Originally a Polytechnic Institute in 1927, it became the first liberal arts college outside the continental United States to receive full accreditation from the Middle States Association of Colleges and Secondary Schools in 1944. Ninety nine percent of the students served by InterAmerican University of Puerto Rico (IAUPR) are Hispanic.

In the late 1950's InterAmerican University of Puerto Rico was the first institution to bring education to the rural areas of the Island by establishing off-campus instructional units. The rapid development of these centers has resulted in the present structure of the university which consists of seven basic units: the Arecibo, Bayamón, San Germán and the Metropolitan Campuses, the Regional Colleges (five), a School of Law, and a School of Optometry. The two main campuses (Metropolitan and San German) offer a full range of undergraduate degrees and a limited number of graduate degrees.

The total enrollment of the University system exceeds 43,000 students making it the largest private university in the nation. A rapid pace in societal changes and technological advances have posed a challenge to constantly improve the quality of its services to the students and to the community.

The Bayamón campus is an autonomous academic unit of Inter American University of Puerto Rico (IAUPR). It was founded in 1956 as an extension of IAUPR, San Germán. The enrollment of the campus totaled approximately 5,000 students in August 1991.

Degrees in the fields of computer, electrican, industrial, and mechanical engineering, electronics and computer technologies, health-related professions, and telecommunications are being created and implemented at the Bayamón campus. The Airway Science program was transferred from the Metropolitan campus to the Bayamón campus in August, 1992. Steps are being taken to insure that first-rate students are attracted to the high technology programs, that a topnotch faculty is recruited, that adequate physical facilities are constructed, and that the curricula reflect the latest advances in technology.

InterAmerican University of Puerto Rico initiated efforts towards the establishment of an Airway Science Program in 1983. To this end, a preliminary analysis was carried out to determine: actual and emerging needs in the local and national job market; student interest and enrollment potential, curriculum requirements, physical plan and instructional equipment required, availability of potential faculty and economic impact. This analysis was carried out with the assistance of the University Aviation Association and the Federal Aviation Administration (FAA).

Federal Aviation Administration approval was received in 1984 to conduct courses in three areas of specialization: Airway Science Management, Airway Computer Science and Airway Electronic Systems. In 1986 a request for approval to curriculum content revision and expansion was submitted to the FAA and in August a fourth area of specialization was established in Aircraft Systems Management.

The program leads to the degree of Bachelor's of Science in Airway Science (B.S. AWS). Graduates have the option of being placed on a register to work for the Federal Aviation Administration (FAA) or work in the private sector. The program demands high standards in admission and graduation requirements to ensure that the quality of the program is maintained. The academic and personal qualifications are determined through written, oral and practical tests administered by the Institution and the Federal Aviation Administration. After the students have satisfactorily approved the credits and requirements for his/her selected major concentration, a Bachelor's degree in Airway Science is conferred.

The Airway Science program has been designed to comply with the Institution's educational goals and to address the following objectives:

1. Development of competent professionals to occupy technical and administrative positions in the field of aviation with the Federal Government and private industry by offering a course of study at the undergraduate levels in four areas of specialization.

2. Provide students with a thorough theoretical background and quality practical experiences in tune with the requirements of society in general and the aviation job market in particular.

3. Maintain an excellent quality of instruction in accordance with FAA requirements and the philosophy and standards of the University.

4. Develop efficient teaching methods in aviation.

5. Foster scientific research studies conducting to improve security and administration in aviation at the local and national level.

6. Promote the dissemination of state-of-the-art technological information related to aviation through collaborative efforts with the regulating agencies and aviation organizations, local as well as international.

7. Offer a continuing education program for aviation professionals.

The Airway Science Management concentration prepares the students to occupy management or administrative positions in the government or private industry. Graduates can obtain positions as air traffic control specialists, managers or administrators for airlines and airports, and general aviation operators, as well as passenger services or cargo agents.

The Airway Electronics Systems concentration offers a comprehensive course of study combining electronics theory with a practical experience. The student can qualify for positions in general aviation manufacturing, NASA, airlines, the Federal Aviation Administration and airline maintenance as well as in the field testing and development as an electronic technician.

In the Airway Computer Science concentration the students learn to operate, design, test and program computers. Work options with the government or private industry as a computer specialist will increase with the advent of new technology in the areas of flight, navigation, communications and information processing.

The Aircraft Systems Management concentrates on flying and is designed to prepare professional pilots with a science and technology background. The student will learn aerodynamics, propulsion systems, aircraft structures and aircraft performance. Graduates from this concentration may obtain commercial pilot license with instruments, multi-engine or flight instructor ratings. They can apply for professional pilot, flight operations manager or flight instructor positions with the private industry and as an aviation safety inspector with the Federal Aviation Administration (FAA).

The requirements for the Bachelor of Science degree in Airway Science include 45 credits of the general Education Program, 27 credits in mathematics, science and technology, 8 credits in computer sciences, 9 credits in management, and 15 credits in aviation, for a total of 104 required credits. In addition, majors in Airway Science Management must take 39 specialization credits for a total of 143 credits, majors in Airway Computer Science take 44 specialization credits for a total of 148 credits, majors in Airway Electronic Systems take 48 credits in specialization for a total of 152 credits, majors in aircraft systems management must take 44 specialization credits for a total of 148 credits.

This Program was established in 1985 with an enrollment of 35 students. By 1986 the enrollment increased to 236 students. The following two years the enrollment progressively increased to 334 students. There was a rapid increase in the years 1989 to 1991 to 567 students. In August 1992 the enrollment decreased abruptly to 358 students. (See Figure 1).

Problem Statement

In this investigation this writer analyzed the factors that determine the desertion of the student in the Airway Science Program at the Interamerican University of Puerto Rico. The desertion of the student was considered, in this case, by all those students that were enrolled in the Airway Science Program and that decided to abandon their studies. With this, I could demonstrate the importance that the educational goals have in the students and how they could be affected by the institutional factors.

Figure 1   Airway Science Program enrollment

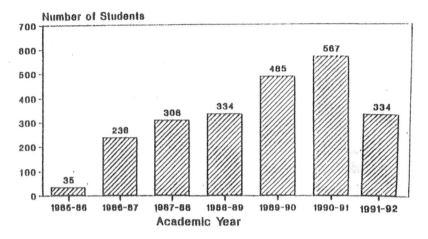

AIRWAY SCIENCES PROGRAM ENROLLMENT
AT INTERAMERICAN UNIVERSITY
OF PUERTO RICO (1985-1991)

This program benefits students from Puerto Rico and the Caribbean. It is the preconception of knowing if the students that decided to abandon the program, did it to meet their academic goals or for some institutional factor or variable that motivated the abandonment.

Purpose of the Study

The purpose of this study was to determine the characteristics of the students that decided to abandon the Airway Science Program of Interamerican University. If they did not meet their goals, what institutional factors influenced in their decision to abandon the Airway Science program?

The present study was oriented to determine what is the perception of the student that decides to abandon the Airway Science Program due to institutional factors and how these affected her/his decision to remain in the university.

Significance of the Study

The decision of abandoning a University institution affects the student, the program and the institution itself.

According to Tinto (1987), a student that decides to abandon the University demonstrates that the quality of the education received does not conform with its expectations. The effectiveness of any educational policy or practice is directly related to the capacity of that policy or practice to increase student involvement in learning (Study Group on the Conditions of Excellence in American Higher Education, 1984). Every institution should accomplish a high satisfaction from the student with the services it offers and the development in the knowledge, affective and psychomotor areas.

If this is not accomplished, the student will decide to abandon the program. In abandoning the program the rate of retention diminishes demonstrating a lesser effectiveness and a congruence does not exist between the objectives established by the program and the product. If this occurs, the university institution is not effective and the evaluation from any accredited agency may be affected. The government funds and economic aids that are offered to an institution are affected if the effectiveness of a program is not shown.

Historically, the Aviation Program at Interamerican University showed a tendency of increasing the number of students enrolled. But that tendency has been decreasing and also the rate of desertion has increased.

The findings of this study were oriented to determine what institutional factors could be determining the increase in the rate of desertion of the students from the Airway Science Program at InterAmerican University.

The results of the study will contribute to serve as predictive in the planning of the College retention Plan. With these findings, a plan of action may be designed and oriented to increase the student retention. It is anticipated that the study will help increase an awareness of the importance of attrition problems among higher education institutions.

Research Questions

What is the relationship between the student's educational plans and goals, institutional factors, and college attrition?

Hypotheses

Hi:1.0

There exists a significant relationship between satisfaction with the institutional factors and the students' attrition.

Hi:2.0

There exists a significant relationship between the students' educational goals and decision in abandoning the Airway Science Program at Interamerican University.

Hi:3.0

There exists a significant relationship between the Grade Point Average at the time that they left the Program and the educational goals of the students that abandoned the Airway Science Program at InterAmerican University.

Assumptions

The following assumptions were established in the study:

-The satisfaction of the students with the institutional factors may affect the decision of the student to abandon the Airway Science Program at Interamerican University.

-Universities are concerned with student attrition.

-Higher Education Institutions may predict student dropout.

-The students' educational goals may affect their decision of abandoning the Airway Science Program at Interamerican University.

-Institutional factors may affect students' persistence

-Students with stable economic resource tend to finish their college education.

Scope and Limitations

With the findings of this investigation it was known how the institutional factors could affect the decision of a student to remain in the Airway Science Program at Interamerican University.

Also, it was established what the goals of a student that enrolls in the Airway Science Program at Interamerican University are and which goals were achieved.

This study was limited because the findings could not be generalized to a population with different characteristics; it could be generalized only to a population with the same characteristics. No empirical evidence existed of similar studies in Puerto Rico.

Delimitations

The scope of the study was limited to a stratified random sample of the students who abandoned the Airway Science Program and the institutional factors of Inter American University.

Operational Definitions of Essential Terms for the Study

Attrition - all those voluntary withdrawals from an institution without formally completing a program. In practice this means that any student not completing a program and not enrolled in the current term after having been enrolled in a past term is counted as contributing to attrition.

Academic Background - all those abilities, skills, and prior schooling the student brings when he starts college.

Educational Goals - the aspirations and projections of the student and changes the student hopes to obtain in his behavior using the education learned in the University.

Environment - the social climate that exists in the institution that induces to study work, and also induces a feeling of belonging and solidarity with the institution.

Institutional Factors - services offered by the institution such as library, financial aid, and counseling.

Retention - permanence of a student in a College Institution until he/she completes his/her study program as determined by the economic, social, ethical and institutional factors.

Satisfaction - number of services the student used and agreed with.

CHAPTER II

REVIEW OF LITERATURE

Introduction

The purpose of this chapter is to review academic research literature pertinent to explaining and understanding the factors related to college students dropping out before graduation. Specifically, the chapter will focus on three kinds of variables central to educational institutions that have been the focus of empirical investigation related to dropping out: (1) teaching, (2) administration, and (3) services, e.g., financial aid and guidance counseling. Following the literature review, the chapter will close with a summary and conclusions.

Studies on the Relationship Between College Student Dropout and Institutional Factors: Teaching, Administration, and Services

Middleton (1987) conducted a study to determine differences in opinion toward selected environmental factors at Ohio University between Black freshmen students who were persisters and those who were dropouts. Based on previous research studies, seven selected environmental factors were determined to be appropriate areas of focus for examining Black freshmen students' opinions of the college environment at Ohio University. The seven selected environmental factors included: (1) student-to-student relations; (2) faculty-to-student relations; (3) student-to-townspeople interaction; (4) student-to-administration relations; (5) social involvement; (6) academic climate; and (7) satisfaction of cultural needs.

An eight-section structured interview instrument was designed by the researcher, tested in a pilot study and utilized in the research process. Structured, in-depth, taped interviews (N=57) were conducted by the researcher. Hypotheses were formulated to make comparisons of persisters' and dropouts' ratings of selected environmental factors: sex, racial mix of the sending high school, socioeconomic background, level of involvement in university-approved organizations, rank in high school graduating class, and college grade point average.

Analysis of variance and Tukey's Test of significance were statistical techniques used to analyze the study data at the .05 level of significance. The results showed that differences in opinions did occur in perceptions of specific selected environmental factors when the groups were compared. The positive view of male dropouts concerning the college environment was a major finding in the research investigation. Overall, the findings indicated that dropouts were more satisfied with the college environment than persisters.

Based on the findings, the researcher made recommendations for the university to take additional steps to help Black students feel a part of overall campus life. These included recruiting more Black faculty, staff and students and conducting workshops to sensitive faculty concerning the racism and hostility black students face in the white college environment.

Olagunju (1981) examined the results of attrition research at Barber Scotia College based on questionnaire responses from 137 students who indicated the degree of their satisfaction with academic and social services provided by the college. Among the significant findings pertinent to the current study, the students who dropped out found the course materials, classroom environment, dormitory living conditions, and financial aid information only partially satisfying; and they found the recreational activities, college regulations, sports equipment, and food services only partially satisfying or dissatisfying.

Based on the findings, the researcher suggested that Barber-Scotia enrollments could be increased and attrition reduced by improving food, health, and recreational services, and also by introducing additional occupational and technical programs, and sending a college recruiter to the public schools to provide information on programs and job opportunities.

Intervention to Improve Student Retention

According to Todd (1986), community colleges have increasingly employed a variety of interventions to improve student retention. When compared to other institutions of higher education, community colleges are cited in retention studies as having the highest student attrition rates: over 50 percent of students drop out by the end of their second year. In his research he found that difficulties with finances have been one of the top three reasons students report for leaving college prematurely. However, they have pointed to the use of finance as perhaps a superficial, socially-acceptable reason for leaving. According to Todd, most retention studies have not dealt directly with the students finance issue, yet the relationship of the student's finances to their successful completion of enrollment objectives is of paramount interest to college administrators, public policy makers, students, and their families.

Todd's study employed analysis using a new conceptual framework for the definition of students' retention. This definition includes the concept of successful student enrollment experience as measured by the student's completion of course work, certificate, and/or degree program. A progress measure was used in the description and comparison of enrollment experiences of aid and no-aid groups. This measure is a combination of number of terms enrolled, cumulative grade point average, and course completion rates. Also, the methodological procedure for determining retention for community college students was further improved by appropriate identification and treatment of dropouts, attrition, and the use of summer terms.

The findings showed financial aid to be a significant factor in retaining students, with particular significance for new freshmen (first time enrolling at the college). Of the total groups, 71 percent of the aid and 61 percent of the no-aid students were enrolled one year later, in the fall term. Between-term attrition rates were more than double for the no-aid group. Financial aid students achieved an average of 3.7 terms of enrollment out of 5, compared to 3.2 for the no-aid group.

Mangum (1985) conducted a study to determine those factors that influence college students to drop out of college. The sample consisted of 403 freshmen day students taking accounting courses, in 1985. The data gathering materials were in two parts: First, a survey composed of questions relating to student perception and satisfaction drawn from the literature; and second, a course evaluation instrument used by the Colleges of Business at Fordham University, New York. The major purpose of the survey (Part I) was to determine if the reasons given by students for dropping out, as reported in the literature, could possibly be used as a predictor for dropouts. The major purpose of the course evaluations (PartII) was to determine if any aspect of teaching, as depicted in the questions of the valuation forms, would have predictive value in determining droputs.

The data were analyzed in three ways: first, using regression analysis; second, using point-biserial correlation; and third, using discriminant analysis. Among the findings it was determined that grade point average, and financial difficulties were statistically significant. From the course evaluation, it was determined that several of the questions evaluating, teaching effectiveness were found to be significant. It was also found that a classification function based on information obtained from the students did accurately pinpoint students dropouts from non-dropouts.

On the basis of the above factors, it is recommended that colleges and universities, which desire to reduce student attrition, devote special attention to the student perceptions regarding teaching effectiveness as well as student financial status and academic performance. One recommendation for further research included following up those students who the models selected as likely to drop out of college but did not drop out.

A second recommendation is that the study should be replicated with two samples, one as control and another to which intervention should be applied.

Nettles, Thoeny, and Gosman (1986) analyzed the relationship between students' performance and, respectively, their race and college experience based on survey responses of 4,094 students (50 percent black, 70 percent White) from 30 U.S. colleges and universities. The criterion variable of performance was the students' cumulative college grade point averages (CCGPAS), and important indicator of whether a student will drop out of college or remain through graduation. The predictor variables in the study were 31 student, faculty, and institutional characteristics. among the variables that were most pertinent for the current study and literature review were general student satisfacftion with the faculty and institution, feelings that the university was nondiscriminatory, and academic integration.

Based on analysis of the data using the Pearson product moment correlation coefficient, multiple analysis of variance, and Chi-square, the researchers found that the strongest predictor variables of CCGPAS at the bivariate level were high-school grade point average, interfering problems, SAT score, age, study habits, academic integration, total enrollment, and socioeconomic status (SES). None of the five faculty scales had a strong relationship with CCGPA. There were four significant interactions with race: SAT scores, student satisfaction, peer group relations, and interfering problems. Black and White students were significantly different in terms of the type of high school attended, their transfer status, gender representation, majority/ minority status, housing patterns, and degree aspirations.

Gille (1985) conducted a study to do the following: (1) test Tinto's model of social and academic integration for predictors of attrition in first time college freshmen, (2) compare scores of freshmen persisters and voluntary dropouts using a previously tested instrument to find which items and factors predict retention in a new population, and (3) compare campus services utilizations of the two groups. The study investigated whether items and scales dealing with students background, extra-curricular activities, faculty relationships, environment, academic and social life, and utilization of campus services could predict persistence.

The total possible data set was 922 fulltime, first time freshmen entering fall 1984 at a middle-sized, public, semirural university in the midwest. Although there were 450 (48.8%) initial responses to the survey instrument, for various reasons the final data set for analysis was 275 to 312. Certain biographic/demographic variables were obtained from a Higher Educational Research Institute form administered to freshmen as they registered. ACT and GPA data were obtained from the Registrar. An instrument utilized in 1981 by Terenzini, Lorang, and Pascarella was used to assess institution characteristics with a new section measuring the utilization of campus services added. The instrument was mailed to respondents in the spring semester.

Principal component factor analysis with varimax rotation was performed on all sections of the survey instrument except that dealing with educatinal outcomes. After regression analysis, only sex and mother's education among the demographic variables were found independently related to persistence; no scales were found to predict persistence independently. This was in constrast to Tinto's model. There seemed to be some support for the Tinto model, since most of the same items in academic and social life loaded together as they had in the TLP studies, although the factor loadings were not as high as previously.

Dropout Models

Bross (1985) conducted a study to develop and test a theoretical model which would help to explain dropping out in adult education. The propositions which were developed to build the theoretical model included the following: (1) Network size, network density and network intimacy are related to persistence; (2) Perceived emotional social support, perceived tangible social support, and perceived informational social support are related to persistence; and (3) Network size, network density and network intimacy are related to feelings of perceived emotional social support, perceived tangible social support and perceived informational social support.

An instrument was developed to determine the size, density and intimacy of each individual's social network, his or her feelings of the three kind of social support, and the individual's age, sex, and highest grade level completed. The outcome variable, persitence, was determined by the number of classes an individual attended before dropping out of the program for reasons other that to take the GED tests. All registered GED students enrolled through the community services divisions of a large, urban, northeastern community college were asked to participate. A total of 104 usable surveys became the final sample size used in the data analysis. Path analysis was used to analyze the data. For the entire sample of 104 individuals, no strong relationships existed between persistence and any of the independent variables.

However, when the data were controlled for all combinations of the three demographic variables' age, sex and grade level completed significant results were obtained. For the subgroup of 40 individuals who were at least 22 years old and had completed at least the tenth grade, network density was significantly and positively related to persistence (beta = .431, p<.05). No other independent variables were significantly related to persistence, although the three support measures demonstrated very high levels of intercorrelation among themselves. Despite the results, Bross claimed that social network and social support may be useful in both understanding persistence and in designing strategies to limit or reduce dropping out.

Gittens (1987) examined the perceptions of students at LaGuardia Community College regarding their experience with cooperative education (CE), a curriculum combining structures work experience and the classroom. Two groups of students were surveyed: students from the class of 1985 who were completing their third and final internship experience; and students from the class of 1981 who dropped out of the college following the completion of at least one internship. The survey sought to determine: (1) the expectations of students on entering the cooperative education program; (2) how their experience differed from expectation; (3) how the internship experience affected their attitudes toward college and their desire to complete their degree; (4) the impact of CE on career goals; (5)

the impact of CE on personal goals; and (6) whether persisters and dropouts differed on the above dimensions.

The questionnaire was adapted from an instrument developed by the New Jersey Equal Opportunity Fund Office for a study of EOF students. It contained both open ended and forced choice questions. The 1981 dropout group in Gittens' study also received a second questionnaire, adapted from an instrument developed for a Nassau Community College study on retention and withdrawal. This instrument elicited information regarding the dropout' reasons for leaving the college and their educational and occupational plans.

Analysis of the data showed that both persisters and dropouts generally reported positive attitudes toward CE. They indicated that the primary advantage of CE was work experience, self confidence, and communication skills. Their exposure to the work environment led most students to raise their levels of educational aspiration to at least a bachelor's degree. However, most planned to complete their degree at LaGuardia before transferring to a senior college. According to Gittens, the study suggested that exposure to work experience is extremely helpful to students in their efforts to achieve self knowledge and self improvement. It further suggested that exposure to the world of work leads many cooperative education students to raise their educational and occupational objectives.

Carroll's (1986) investigation focused primarily on the determinants of academic success and dropout behavior in a predominantly Black urban community college. A questionnaire was developed by the researcher, based on earlier research findings on student retention and attrition. A total of 137 Black college freshmen from two different programs participated in this study. Groups of persisting, dropout, and transfer students were identified in each program population. The data was analyzed using correlational analysis, discriminant analysis and analysis of variance.

The findings revealed that two variables; highest expected degree and perceived counselor guidance effectiveness; were especially important in distinguishing those who dropped out from those who succeeded. High school average was not a very good predictor of dropout or success status. Students who were pursuing less than a bachelor's degree had most negative attitudes toward their freshman college experience. Generally, three measures of students' attitudes toward their college experience peer group associations, student/ faculty interactions, and student/counselor interactions were strictly related to student outcome. In addition, distance of the college from home, English as a first language, and specification of the college as the student's first choice prior to admission also significantly related to freshman attrition in the urban community college. Results supported the importance of adequate counseling to student outcome, and to the students' attitudes about their educational experience.

Kaliszeski (1986) attempted to determine if there was a significant difference involving selected students characteristics between students who followed the "cooling out" process and those who did not as measured by their graduation status from a two year community college. The cooling out process was defined as a counseling strategy designed to assist students with unrealistic aspirations in selecting alternative career goals which would be more in line with their abilities.

The sample drawn for this study was taken from two community colleges in Florida. The criterion was that one served a predominantly urban population and one served a predominantly rural population. From each college a master list of students was obtained whose last term of enrollment was the Fall semester 1984. From these lists a total of 100 dropouts and 100 graduates were randomly selected for study. An ex post facto design was utilized which involved collecting certain information for each student in the sample by reviewing academic transcripts. Additional information was obtained through a subsequent telephone interview. Data which were collected concerning race, gender, father's occupation, status (dropout or graduate), and process (followed the cooling out process or did not follow the cooling out process) were synthesized for each student and recorded for analysis. Non- parametric statistical procedures were performed to determine if significant differences existed between student status and process based on the variables of race, gender, and father's occupation.

Results of the study showed (a) the relationship between student status and the cooling out process was statistically significant; it appeared to be linked to dropping out or graduating regardless of race, gender, or father's occupation.

LeBlanc (1986) conducted a study to examine student dropout patterns in the California community colleges as perceived by counselors of the various colleges surveyed. Their views were held by the researcher to be useful for the development of programatic strategies and procedures for ensuring greater student retention.

The methodology of the study was descriptive. A total population of 106 head counselors was surveyed. The data collected were interpreted by utilizing the percentage of response, frequency of response, and the means of the population surveyed. The findings from the study showed that the counselors surveyed perceived dropout as student who primarily enrolled in part time programs, and whose major reasons for dropping out were job hours/class conflict, and lack of finances.

Further, according to the counselors surveyed, the majority of dropouts are "stopouts", i.e., they intend to resume their education. Sixtysix percent of the counselors replied that their dropouts planned to return to college at a later date.

Based on the findings, the primary recommendation offered by LeBlanc was that students should be encouraged to seek counseling prior to a final decision to stopout of community college. She also recommended that the Community Colleges create enrollment management committees to determine the rate of stopout retention in their college, and to develop programs geared towards greater student retention.

Williamson (1986) conducted a study to determine the extent to which Tinto's model of the dropout process applied to a national sample of community college students. Strict definitions of persistence were used in applying a Tinto-based model to both the 2 and 4 year student samples from the High School and Beyond (HSB) data set. The primary focus of the study was to determine the relative effects of social and academic integration in relation to student background characteristics, on two measures of persistence in the institution, and persistence in higher education.

The data were analyzed using path analyses procedures. The major findings of the study revealed that: (1) student background characteristics may be more influential than institutional characteristics in explaining the long term persistence behavior of students, (2) background variables directly affected persistence, no matter how defined, (3) the ability of Tinto's model to explain persistence may be highly dependent on the criteria used in defining persistence, and (4) the Tinto model may better explain institutional persistence than persistence in the system of higher education.

Retention Programs

Robinson (1989) compared retention rates and grade point averages (GPAS) of high risk freshmen who participated in an 8 week transition to college orientation course with those of (1) a control who did not take the course and (2) the entire freshman class. The subjects were classified as high risk if their American College Test scores were lower than the class mean. In fall 1986, there were 61 subjects in the orientation classes, 15 controls, and 700 in the freshmen class. In fall 1987, there were 137 subjects in the orientation class and 19 controls. Retention rates of high risk students who took the orientation course and the control group were about the same. Thus, the course did not have a positive effect on retention rates; and since the study also showed that both of these groups experienced higher attrition rates than the total freshman class, this suggests that, at least for the experimental group, the course could have, somehow, even contributed to higher attrition.

Lee (1988) analyzed seven student retention programs at 93 smaller community colleges, including their use, cost, staffing, and cost-effectivenes. The findings from the study suggested that peer-related and adult learner interventions may be useful in preventing attrition. Further, Lee's study presented data to indicate that certain programs may be specially effective for preventing attrition among adult learners, including programs dealing with adult learner reintegration, peer tutoring and counseling, remedial development, career planning, and student support and integration.

Mallinckrodt (1988) conducted a trend study of 101 White and 42 Black college undergraduates to analyze the relationship between persistence at college and preceptions of social support from the campus community and family. After a year, the researcher found that, among the subjects, 24 White and 10 Black students had dropped out. Comparing these students to those who remained in school in relationship to the perceptual data collected, the researcher reported that the results suggested that social support was an important factor in retention. Support from members of the campus community appeared crucial for Black subjects, while family support was most important for White subjects. The results of the study also suggested that it could be possible to identify both Black and White students at risk for dropping out, using a brief self report screening inventory.

Giddan, Levy, Estroff & Cline (1987) analyzed the relationship between individual counseling or psychotherapy and short term student retention rates at an urban university. Changes in attendance rates, such as dropping out or returning between quarters were used to evaluate program effects. In Giddan's study, attendance patterns of 1,290 counseled students were compared with 1,221 non counseled, base rate undergraduates. The findings showed that 75 percent of upper class men reported conceivable retention advantages of receiving counseling center services over the base rate group. Freshmen results, however, suggested that counseling was associated with student attrition, not retention.

Wilder (1983), based on his examination of factors that influence college students to forego their educational pursuits, i.e., drop out, proposed that well conceived and carefully conceptualized programs of retention are essential if higher education is to hold on to its students. Because of the importance attributed to positive student faculty relationship, he argued, new ways must be devised by the college or university community to maximize interaction between the faculty and students. Retention demands that the total higher education community (academic affairs, business affairs, institutional advancement, and student affairs) work together; optimal benefits will be gained only if effective programs of retention are executed cooperatively. Wilder concluded that institutions that fail to develop effective programs of student retention will not be able to offset the enevitable losses of enrollment resulting from the dwindling college bound pool.

Gosman (1983), in a study of college student retention and progression, found significant differences between Black and White student cohorts in terms of their attrition rates, overall progression rates (defined as length of time to graduate), and tendency to follow the prescribed progression pattern (sophomore in the 2nd year, junior in the 3rd year, senior in the 4th year, and graduate after the 4th year). However, multiple regression analysis showed that racial differences disappeared when the effects of other students and institutional characteristics were statistically controlled, including financial aid services, type of institution (private or public), percentage of nonwhites in the school, and family socioeconomic background. Therefore the authors concluded that college and university administrators should re-think the nature of special retention and counseling programs especially designed to serve minority group students.

Carroll (1988) examined whether participation in a college discovery program was useful in the retention of 137 educationally under-prepared Black freshmen. Seventythree of the subjects participated in the Discovery Program, which involved individual and group counseling. As defined by Carrol, the dependent variables in the study were (1) continuous full-time enrollment in the 1st year, and (2) academic dropout. The independent variables in the study were peer interactions, Student counselor interactions, and student/ faculty interactions. Based on analysis of the data, Carrol reported the results showed that perceived counselor guidance was the best single predictor for these subjects; the more the students perceived they were obtaining beneficial counsellor guidance, the less likely they were to drop out of college. In addition, Carrol found that the nature and frequency of both student/faculty and student/peer interactions were strongly related to whether or not the subjects dropped out during their first year or displayed continuous full time enrollment.

Rysberg (1986) was interested in examining dropping out in relationship to the type of teaching method college students received. For the study, the researcher used students enrolled in an introductory psychology course, 550 of whom received traditional lecture based instruction and 232 of whom received a modified format. The latter included the following five elements: (1) the instructor's pacing, (2) unit mastery, (3) the use of student proctors, (4) written words as secondary forms of instruction, and (5) lectures as primary forms of instruction.

Based on a comparison of the subjects' performance, the researcher found that those students given the modified format had a lower dropout rate than subjects in the traditional course. Specifically, in the traditional course format, 6.7 percent of the students dropped out where as in the modified format only 3.1 percent of the students dropped out. In addition, the researcher found that those students exposed to the modified format performed significantly better and rated the course significantly more positively than students given the traditional format.

Dropout Rates of Minority Students

Spaights, Dixon and Nickolai (1985) analyzed conditions that likely contribute to the high dropout rate from schools of higher education of minority students, specially Black students. The researchers, after pointing out that over the past several decades an increasing number of Black have been entering post-high school educational institutions, also emphasized that these are often traditionally White institutions, and that there is an unwitting racism in these schools that contributes to the high Black students attrition rate. Of particular relevance to this literature review, the authors pointed out the negative effects of administrative nonsupport and faculty misconceptions and stereotypes of the students. With respect to the administration, the authors noted, among other things, that the White administrators often failed to create policies that produced a meaningful higher educational experience for the Black students, especially by ignoring their unique cultural heritage in the curriculum. With respect to the faculty, the authors emphasized that they hold the key to whether or not students remain in the educational institution, since they do the grading. If they do not understand the needs of their students, or if they are secretly afraid of their students, because of racist attitudes they hold, they will ignore the needs of Black students in the course readings and lectures. This, in turn, will create a negative or irrelevant educational experience for the Black students, and increase the chance that they will drop out of college.

Given the reality of these and other factors in many higher educational institutions that cause or contribute to a high dropout rate among Black students, the authors arque that changes in the thinking and policies of White administrators and faculty must come about before Black students can be expected to fare better at traditionally White colleges and universities.

Tambe (1984) evaluated 32 variables, pertinent to Tinto's theory of drop out from college, he thought would predict whether an open admission student continued college work or dropped out immediately after acceptance at Virginia State University. The 32 variables, which included, for example, SAT scores, family SES, guidance counsellor evaluations, and the student's degree of commitment to the university, were grouped by the researcher into categories involving personal characteristics, family background characteristics, and institutional characteristics. Tambe hypothesized that the outcomes of persistence (continued enrollment) or withdrawal (dropout) would be a functional of academic ability, goal and institutional commitment, and expected degree of academic and social integration at college. The criterion measures of the study consisted of student enrollment status persistor or dropout at the end of the 1979-1980 academic year.

In order to test his hypotheses, Tambe collected data from 185 open admissions freshmen admitted in 1978 and from 240 such students admitted in 1979. Based on discriminant analysis for the 32 predictor variables and the two student criterion categories, Tambe unfortunately had to report that the results indicated a lack of uniformity and little discriminatory power. Only three of the 32 variables were significant, including reading scores, degree of academic preparation, and anticipation of needing extra time to meet degree requirements, but none of these were significant for both groups studied. The researcher thus concluded that accurate predictions of persistence and withdrawal for individual students admitted to college by open admissions policies cannot be made at the time of matriculation.

Glennen (1985), in a study of an intrusive advising system utilizing faculty advisors working with a large minority population, found a sizeable reduction in the attrition of minorities, an increase in the number of minority graduates, an increase in the number of minorities achieving dean's list, and an increase in minority employment after graduation. From the study, Glennen concluded that the intrusive advisement system helped minority students identify and cope with academic and personal problems early so that the problem did not interfere with normal academic progress.

Kowalski (1982) examined both personal and academic characteristics he thought might be related to dropping out or persisting in college. His sample of subjects included 201 persisting and 165 nonpersisting university students. Based on analysis of data involving personal characteristics of students, student/faculty relationships, and institutional factors, Kowalski found that the following variables pertinent to this study influenced the dropout rate: (1) student dissatisfaction with the general atmosphere at school, (2) poor student/faculty relationships, (3) perception of the university or college as failing in its purposes. The researcher also found these variables to be related to dropping out: (4) parental pressure and familiar problems. (5) lack of interest in school work, (6) lack of basic academic skills, (7) a general sense of discouragement and unhappiness.

Attrition Beyond the Freshmen Year

Carter (1986) explored attrition in a more extended fashion than in typical in the literature by examining attrition beyond the freshmen year. The research was based primarily on the model developed by Vincent Tinto in 1975. Tinto argued that the process of dropout from college is a longitudinal process of interaction between the individual and the academic and social systems of the college, which leads to continuous modification of goal and institutional commitments in ways that affect persistence and/or dropout behavior. The general notion is that the higher the degree of integration of the individual into the college system, the greater will be his or her commitment to the institution and to the goal of graduation.

The purpose of Carter's investigation was two-fold. The first was to test Tinto's model of attrition, using a sample of sophomore, junior, and senior students from a large, public, prestigious university. The second purpose was to add another variable to the Tinto model, curricular integration, and to examine its relation to attrition at these levels. A questionnaire was developed by the researcher and distributed to randomly selected sample of approximately 2,300 persisters currently enrolled sophomore, junior, and senior students from a large, midwestern university. The survey was also distributed to approximately 1,500 nonpersisters, all students who did not return to the university for the fall term of 1986 after having enrolled in the fall of 1985, and who did not receive a degree.

The major findings were that: (1) the basic constructs of the Tinto model contributed significantly to the differentiation between persisters and nonpersisters in a fashion consistent with the Tinto theory; (2) there was some variation in the degree of importance of these variable sets as a function of academic class level, as hypothesized; (3) the measures of social and academic integration consisted of several dimensions which relate differently to attrition; (4) the curricular integration variable set proved to be an important contributor to explained variance in persistence/withdrawal behavior at all academic levels, with more curricularly integrated students; and (5) student's stated reasons for leaving school differentiated between persisters and nonpersisters equally as well or better than major constructs of the Tinto model.

Students Persistence and Performance

Trippi and Baker (1989), investigated the correlates of students persistence and performance among 117 Black male and 193 Black female freshmen attending a predominantly White Northeastern University. The dormitory arrangements provided for the students was the service variable studied that had the most relevance for the current study. From the analysis, the researchers found that several variables were significantly related to persistence as well as performance among Black women, including the characteristics of their roommates, the racial composition of the residence hall unit, and the high school grade performance of their roommates. Regarding the characteristics of the residence hall for Black women, those who had residence in a hall where there were many other Black students performed the best.

Performance and Dropouts

Tota (1986), conducted a study to analyze improved student achievement and decreased dropout rates in Roanoke, Virginia, viewed through goal and policy adoption and implementation. The research method employed was the case study method involving analysis of ex post facto conditions. Reports on student performance and dropouts as mandated by the State Department of Education were analyzed in terms of student ability, grade level equivalents, and droputs and suspensions compared to local unemployment rates. A typology of perspectives was used to identity reform, to report legislated change, and to describe implemented educational programs. Data regarding School Board adopted policies and goals were collected from the official School board policy manual, School Board minutes and publications, and the National School boards Association's policy and research reports. A comparison of the instructional policy area researched by the National School Boards Association (NSBA) relevant to effective schools and those instructional policies and goals adopted by the Roanoke City School Board revealed a correlation of 88 percent between the NSBA policies listed and policies adopted by the School Board. Policies and goals dealing with student performance and dropouts on a district wide basis, adopted publicly by the School board, yielded improved results.

The results of the study indicated improved student performance and a decrease in the student dropout rate in all schools in the district as a result of School board policy and goal formation and implementation. According to the researcher, critical reform, legislated change, planning, implementation, and outcome must be considered as interrelated elements if performance is to improve and be maintained. While most policies regarding dropouts deal with attendance, those policies most likely to affect the dropout rate deal with guidance, teaching techniques, alternative education, and personnel.

Retention Systems

White and Shahan (1989), were interested in the effect of a retention systems at Lamar University, Port Arthur, in Texas, designed to encourage entering freshmen to remain in college rather than drop out. As explained by the reseachers the education reform movement in Texas has included a state mandate that demands that all college freshmen in Texas pass the texas Academic Skills Test. The Lamar University, Port Arthur faculty, staff, and administration developed a student motivation and retention system at admissions time to identify the academic strengths and weaknesses, as well as personal social characteristics, of each student. A faculty advisor system was established to meet weekly with each freshmen and provide guidance. In addition, a learning center with extensive instructional systems and developmental courses and tutoring added to the retention management system.

Based on the researchers' preliminary analysis of the data, the results showed that the percentage of freshmen entering in January 1989 and remaining for at least eight weeks was 15 percent higher than that for the previous January, and that the percentage of freshmen entering in the fall of 1989 and remaining at least eight weeks was 20 percent higher than the previous fall. Thus it was concluded that there was a positive effect on retention of the faculty advisor retention system, the learning center,and factors related to these.

In "Attrition '89: A survey of non-returning students in spring 1989" (1989), the results are reported of a survey conducted of Cumberland Country College (CCC) students who enrolled in fall 1988 but did not return in spring 1989. Questionnaires were mailed to all 718 nonreturning students, requesting information on their educational goals, enrollment patterns, ratings of college services, reasons for not returning, and personal characteristics. Among the findings from the study, based on a 34.5 percent response rate of the nonreturning students, were the following: (1) in comparison to CCC graduates, nonreturning students made less use of college support services and gave them lower rating; (2) six percent reported dissatisfaction with course offerings; (3) 83 percent were enrolled part time; (4) 58 percent had employed related goals, and 71 percent were employed full time while attending school; (5) 16 percent gave financial reasons for not returning; and (6) in comparison with nonreturning students form previous years, fewer 1988-89 nonreturning students dropped out because they had transferred or because they had achieved their goals.

A study by Meznek (1989) described the Puente Project, a statewide program that helps Mexican American/Latino community college students in California achieve their academic goals. Puente's goals are to reduce the number of Mexican American/Latin community college students who drop out of school and increase the number who transfer to four year institutions. To meet these goals, the project trains English teachers and Mexican American counselors to work as teams in conducting one year writing/counseling/mentoring programs for Mexican American/Latino students. Since Puente began at Chabot College in 1982, 18 other California community colleges have initiated Puente programs on their campuses and over 1,800 students have been served. The programs have been monitored on student a regular basis, and data have been collected each year on student enrollments, retention, and transfer.

Analysis of these data, while not directly reporting on dropping out, provided results for many performance indicators related to dropping out, which suggested that students participating in the Puente Project would have lower dropout rates than otherwise might be expected for this population. Among the findings were that 83 percent of the students who enrolled in Puente successfully completed the developmental writing class; 72 percent of those who went on to take English 1A completed it; and a total of 134 Puente students trasferred to a state or private university. According to Meznek, the program's success can be attributed to the collaboration between English teachers and Mexican American counselors, research-base writing methods, culturally based academic counseling, an exemplary training model with ongoing staff development, strong community-based support, and a working partnership among community groups, postsecondary institutions, philanthropic organizations, and corporations.

Attrition of Hearing Impaired Students

Walter (1987), conducted a survey of 145 postsecondary programs for hearing-impaired students in North America, to study attrition rates. Estimated attrition rates were found to be lowest for the group of programs primarily offering Diplomas, with a rate of 59 percent, and highest for those offering Associate degrees, with a rate of 79 percent. Open ended interviews were conducted with 20 students who transferred from a mainstream postsecondary program to the National Technical Institute for the Deaf. Three reasons were identified to explain the students' withdrawal from their first college: inability to communicate with teachers, inadequate support services, and limited opportunities for social interaction with peers. It was concluded by the researchers that accommodations to meet the special needs of hearing-impaired learners may not be adequate to ensure their graduation, and a reason for the high rates of attrition may be a lack of social and academic integration of hearing-impaired students into mainstreamed college life.

Attrition on Persisting and Non-Persisting Students

Airhart (1987), added to the research on community college level attrition by comparison persisiting and non-persisting students. The study instrument utilized the Tinto conceptual Dropout Schema. Fortysix items related to the following factors derived from Tinto: family background, individual attributes, past educational experiences, goal commitment, and academic/social integration.

Freshman level community college students were surveyed within intact history classes during the Fall semester. The following semester, respondents were classified as either dropouts or persisters (dropout status). Persisters had re-enrolled in the college for the Spring semester, and dropouts had not re-enrolled. Initially, a chi square analysis was utilized to determine if significant relationships existed between individual variables and dropouts status. There was a significant relationship between dropout status and age, time attending classes, number of courses taken, number of hours in class per week, type of program in which enrolled, high school curriculum, highest grade completed, high school rank, hours working per week, plans for a four-year degree, and highest degree envisioned from college.

Following the chi square analysis, a discriminant function analysis was conducted to find, if possible, a subset of predictor variables that would significantly discriminate between dropout and persister groups. All 46 items from the original questionnaire were entered as variables in the analysis. These nominal variables which were not dichotomous in nature were reformulated as dummy variables. Conducted in three phases, the discriminant function analysis did retain a group of predictor variables that significantly discriminated between dropouts and persisters (p=.00010). The discriminant function equation resulting from the analysis correctly classified 77 percent of the persisters and 64 percent of the dropouts. A post hoc analysis demonstrated that end of semester GPAs increased classification of persisters and dropouts to 87 percent and 80 percent, respectively. A follow-up study on a sample of dropouts and persisters revealed a significant dependent relationship between three variables and dropout status. These variables were commitment to college completion, need for more guidance in choosing a major, and a need for supervision in course selection.

Integration and Involvement Among Chicano Students

VonDestinon (1988), was interested in dropping out among Chicano students, and conducted an extensive review of theory, focusing on the theories of Tinto and Astin regarding student integration and involvement, as well as studies on the topic. From his research, VonDestinon identified Chicano student characteristics corresponding closely to those variables influences attrittion hypothesized by Tinto. Chicano students, for example, reported being poorly prepared by their high schools for college. Also, of particular relevance for the current study, services provided by the institution and interactions with faculty were two areas which helped contribute to persistence or attrition. Their social integration into the institutional enviromental also contributed to their persistence, along with family support.

Finances emerged as critical in the persistence decision, primarily due to the low socio economic status of the Chicano population.

Student Tutoring

Koehler (1984), in order to evaluate the effectiveness and value of the tutoring provided by the University of Cincinnati's Tutorial and Referral Services, collected data on the success of students tutored during the 1978-79 school year and on their subsequent retention. Student success was analyzed by race, sex, age, and college. Data for 487 tutored and 284 nontutored students were analyzed. Attrition and grade data were isolated for all groups, and cost efficiency was examined by determining the number of students saved by the program (calculated by substracting the percentage of tutored students who left school from the percentage ofnontutored students who left school and multiplying that percentage by the number of students tutored). The savings generated by the program in terms of tuition, student activity fees, and the full-time equivalence subsidy from the state were then calculated.

Analyses of the student data revealed that 45.1 percent of the nontutored group in 1978-79 failed to enroll for the autum quarter in 1979-80, where as just 20.3 percent of the tutored group failed to enroll. Tutoring was found to have made a substancial difference in the retention of older students, black and white males.

Wilder (1983), in spring 1984, conducted a three-part withdrawal study al Glendale (Arizona) Community College (GCC) to investigate reasons for both course withdrawal and oficial and unofficial college withdrawal. Based on analysis of responses from 138 students who withrew from courses, 282 students who officially withdrew from GCC, and 9 students who left courses without officially withdrawing, the researcher reported the following: (1) major reasons given by males for withdrawing from courses were conflicting job hours, course loads that were too heavy, and grade problems, while the two major reasons given by females were dissatisfaction with instruction and conflicting job hours, followed by course loads that were too heavy and personal/family reasons; (2) over 94 percent of the students who withdrew from courses felt that consulting with a counselor would not have beneficial with respect to their decision to withdraw; (3) both males and females, the major reason for withdrawing from GCC were conflicting job hours; (4) 70 percent of the males and 67 percent of the females who withdrew from GCC planned to return the following fall; (5) 90 percent of the withdrawing males and 75 percent of the females were employed; (6) 40 percent of the withdrawing males and 47 percent of the females had used counseling services; and (7) the major reasons given by students who stopped attending classes without withdrawing were dissatisfaction with instruction, conflicting job hours, and dissatisfaction with course content.

Brophy (1986), conducted a follow-up study at Sierra College (California) to determine why students who dropped out of all of their classes during fall 1984 left the college. The dropout population included 1,549 students, of whom only 374 (27 percent) returned to college in spring 1985. A survey instrument was sent to all withdrawing students, requesting information on personal characteristics; educational, social, cultural, and personal goals; educational background; academic major; college choice; grade point average; course load; employment; academic; financial, and other reasons for withdrawing from college; awareness and use of college services; educational attitudes; and perceptions of Sierra College.

The findings from the study, based on 400 usable responses and comparisons with findings from a 1981 retention study, included the following: (1) profile characteristics were the same for 1981 and 1984, with the "typical" dropout likely to be a Caucasian or Hispanic, middle-age, married, female, taking one class for three or fewer units for a vocational or recreational purposes, with no intention of transferring; (2) first-time students withdrew at a lesser rate in 1984 than in 1981; (3) 39.9 percent of the 1984 group withddrew in the first two and one-half weeks of the semester; (4) over half declared general studies as their major; (5) 46 percent of the 1984 group had attended college before; 6) 50 percent of the 1984 group knew of college services but did not use them; and (7) personal reasons were most frequently cited for leaving college, followed by academic and financial reasons.

Student Attrition and Retention

Marinaccio (1985), pointed out that student attrition and retention have been familiar terms in higher education for a long time, but that only recently has there developed an increased awareness of the cost of attrition, both to students and to community colleges. Although research has not provided any solutions of the complex problem of attrition, studies have identified some basic characteristics that appear to be linked with attrition and retention at the community college. Among the student characteristics affecting attrition areacademic factors (e.g., student's previous academic attainment), demographic factors, students' motivations and aspirations, and financial considerations. Institutional characteristics influencing attrition include the size and services of the college, student involvement, and institutional policies and procedures. The dominant theme in retention research is that retention and attrition result from the interactions that take place between the student and the institution.

According to Marinaccio, steps to improve these interactions that can apply to virtually any type of institution include the following: (1) establish an institution-wide retention steering committee; (2) determine the dropout rate; (3) conduct a study to determine why students are leaving; (4) conduct an institutional self-study to determine where improvements are necessary and where the institution is successful; and (5) institute a tangible reward system for good teaching and faculty advising.

In a "Study of Attrition among students at LaGuardia Community College" (1983), conducted during 1980-82, it is explained that the study was conducted to determine why students left LaGuardia Community College (LCC) before completing the requirements for an associate degree. Interviews were conducted with dropouts students over the course of the study, and questionnaires were administered to entering and continuing students to provide a comparative framework. The study focused on reasons for withdrawal, current activities of dropouts, demographic and educational characteristics of dropouts and continuing students, attitudes toward LCC, academic plans and expectations, work and finances the cooperative education program, academic ability and basics skills courses, studying, homework, consultation with teachers, freshman seminar, use of services and assistance at LCC, suggestions for dropout prevention, and anticipated social life at LCC.

Based on an analysis of the data, the findings from the study included the following: (1) a relatively small number of motives explained dropping out for the majority of students, with various personal problems (e.g., family problems, health, pregnancy, and/or marriage) accounting for just over half of all withdrawals; (2) other reasons for students dropping out included characteristics of the school itself (specially lack of specific programs); (3) additional factors explaining dropping out included poor motivation, career choices that did not need college-level study, and academic deficiencies; (4) 23 percent of the dropouts enrolled in other educational programs; (4) LCC dropouts and continuing students did not differ either on demographic variables or on measures of past educational performance or ability; and (5) students who left LCC were less likely to have financial aid or paternal assistance and more likely to work full-time than continuing students.

Rounds (1983), conducted a study at Cerritos College to gain a better understanding of students who dropped all of their clases. The study involved exit surveys administered as part of the official dropout process, exit surveys used during the graduation check process, and an analysis of institutional data on the personal and academic characteristics of spring 1983 students. Results were compared with findings from a similar study conducted in 1980.

The findings from the study, based on survey responses from 376 dropouts and 268 graduates, included the following: (1) students dropped out due to job conflict, personal reasons, illness, or general dissatisfaction; (2) 26 percent of the dropouts originally came to Cerritos to prepare for transfer, 26 percent to train for a job, 23 percent to explore a new career or subject, and 18 percent for self-enrichment; (3) since spring 1980, dropouts' values had become more pragmatic and less humanitarian; (4) dropouts consistently attributed less value to educational outcomes than graduates; (5) 67 percent of the dropouts felt well prepared by the college and 70 percent were very satisfied with the instruction they received; (6) graduates were more familiar and more satisfied with support services than dropouts;

(7) 94 percent of the dropouts said they would recommend Cerritos to another student; (8) 61 percent of the dropouts did not feel they had achieved their goals while at Cerritos; and (9) compared to graduates, dropouts more frequently tended to enroll full-time, be new or re-admitted students, be older females, and have fewer units earned.

Attrition During Freshman and Sophomore Year

Nelson and Urff (1982), investigated reasons accounting for attrition of University of North Dakota (UND) students. UND students who were enrolled during fall 1976-1977 through fall 1979-1980 as new freshmen and who terminated their studies without earning a degree between spring 1978-1979 to fall 1979-1980 were surveyed. The 237 respondents represented a response rate of 32.9 percent. The American College Testing Program's Withdrawing/Nonreturning Student Survey was administered. Respondents were typically female (60.7 percent) and between the ages of 20 and 25 years (84.4 percent).

Analysis of the data showed that the decision to leave the university typically occurred during the freshman or sophomore year. The respondents who left UND prior to earning a degree indicated that the primary reason was to attend a different college or because they wanted to move. Major factors underlying the decision to attend a different college included (1) the desired major not being offered, and (2) dissatisfaction with a variety of other aspects of the institution, including the faculty. The decision to move seemed to be primarily related to travel desires. Although students generally reported satisfaction with the services and characteristics of UND (as well as with their decision to enroll), some potential areas for improvement were identified. It was found that three of the nine areas of least satisfaction concerned academic advising. It was also found that 27.4 percent of the respondents were dissatisfied with the concern shown for them as individuals.

More than one fourth of the respondents did not know about campus programs and services that might have helped them in the decision to transfer, withdraw, or remain in school. Four of every 10 left without formally withdrawing.

From the study, the researchers concluded that dissatisfaction with certain university functions may have influenced student decisions to leave UND, and that a positive change in the attitude of faculty and staff toward students and improvement in the quality of academic advising may help to improve the retention rate in the future.

Hellmich (1989), claimed that in spite of difficulties in analyzing student retention in community college programs and courses, certain facts about student attrition are known. First, students who drop out of class or school tend to have lower grades than students who persist. Second, the ability of students to drop in and out of community colleges at will has negative effects on the curriculum. Third, High attrition rates are evidence of a college's failure to socialize its students into the academic and social norms of the institution. Fourth, high attrition is likely to be associated with low faculty morale. Finally, for the many students who are ill-prepared for the academic rigors of college, withdrawal may be an appropriate action. Drawing form these assumptions, Santa Fe Community College's English Department develop a series of recommendations for a departmental retention plan to reduce high in-class attrition rates in introductory English classes. These recommendations stressed that the retention program must emerge from the department as a whole and urged the department to do the following: (1) instigate a thorough demographic analysis of students attrition within specific English courses; (2) augment the academic advising of targeted student populations; (3) examine methods of increasing students/ instructor out-of-class contact without overburdening instructors; (4) draw upon the expertise of its instructors to gather pedagogical devices for enhancing student participation within the classroom; (5) integrate sections of the targeted course(s) with sections from other disciplines; (6) enforce a strict class attendance policy; (7) increase the number of honors courses in English; and (8) evaluate quantitatively and qualitatively the effectiveness of its retention program at the end of each term and formally present these results to the college administration.

McClain and Sartwell (1983), studied reasons for the withdrawal of 159 first-semester freshmen from Sale, State College, Massachusetts, during the fall 1981 or 1982 semesters. The study rested on the following assumptions: (1) not getting into the dorm contributes to attrition for some students, (2) the registration process discourages some students, (3) community problems contribute to student withdrawal, (4) financial problems play an important role in student withdrawal, (5) some students are not ready for college.

Based on analysis of the questionnaire data collected, the researchers found the following; the greatest frequency of official withdrawal occurred for business administration students and students who had not declared a major; 62 percent of the withdrawing students indicated that Salem State College was their first college choice; two thirds of the respondents were enrolled in the major of their choice; 78 percent withdrew without meeting with their advisor prior to withdrawal; 64 percent were employed, but only 18 percent worked more than 20 hours per week; 70 percent contributed toward the costs of attending college; and 50 percent of students who withdrew indicated that they had transferred to another college.

Summary and Conclusions

A relatively large amount of research has been carried out to attempt to determine the factors related to college students dropping out before graduation. This research has focused heavily on community colleges and Black students, though drop out at four year colleges and among students of all ethnic backgrounds have also received significant attention. Much of the research on drop out among college students has considered institutional factors related to teaching, administration, and services, the focus of the literature review and current dissertation study.

Collectively, these studies have shown that a wide variety of factors are significantly related to drop out, including factors pertaining to teaching, administration, and services. However, few if any studies cite these as the only factors related to dropout, or attempt to distinguish how much weight these factors carry in a student's decision to drop out relative to personal, family background, and other factors. In addition, it is rare to find a study involving the variables of primary concern to this literature review that related such variables to the different types of drop out behavior, including dropping out to transfer, dropping out temporarily, and dropping out permanently, among others.

From the research on drop out, it does appear clear, however, that students are less likely to drop out the more positive their experience with their instructors, both in the classroom and on an interpersonal level; the more the administration's policies and procedures satisfy their educational as well as cultural needs; and the more that services provided by the educational institution, specially guidance counseling and financial aid, alleviate or eliminate personal and financial problems.

Separating these dimensions of the educational experience for students, however teaching, administrative policies and procedures, and services may be more of a conceptual exercise than a reality; for when students are in school, they are apt to experience all aspects of the educational process as interrelated, not discrete. In addition, services provided by the college or university are usually determined by administrative policies, so that the former is really an outgrowth or aspect of the latter. Further, ineffective or even harmful policies of the administration can cause low morale among all members of the educational community, including the instructional staff. This, in turn can affect the quality of teaching and teacher-student relation; thus even teacher related variables can be seen to be dependent, to a greater or lesser extent, on administrative policies.

Based on this type of reasoning, it might be wise for researchers interested in student drop to take more of a systems approach to the phenomenon, considering the relationship between and among the institutional variables, and further, considering how these are modified by personal and family variables. Conducting this type of study, however, is difficult for most researchers, specially those in graduate programs, who have limited resources involving time and finances. Despite the practical and conceptual problems involved in systems research, it is important to remember that when a student decides to drop out of college, the explanation may be highly complex, the results of the interaction of many factors.

Perhaps one day researchers will identify a few key variables that predict with high probability which student or group of students will drop out of college, and when they will do this. This would benefit all concerned by simplifying what appears to be, as mentioned, a highly complex phenomenon. With these considerations in mind, this study will attempt to further clarify the effect of institutional factors involving teaching, administration, and services on drop out among college students.

CHAPTER III
METHODOLOGY

Introduction

The primary purpose of this work is to study the factors associated with the improvement of student retention in the Airway Science Program at Interamerican University of Puerto Rico.

This section includes a description of the population and selection of the sample of the study, description of the instrument, delimitations of the study, research procedures and statistical procedures for the analysis of the data.

Population

The population of this study was constituted by 434 (98 female; 336 male) students that decided to abandon the Airway Science Program at InterAmerican University.

Selection of the Sample

A representative sample was selected from the population. The sample was stratified by gender. It was constituted by 34 (8%) female students and 118 (27%) male students. Table 1 shows that a sample of 152 students representing 35% was selected at random from the population.

Table 1   Population and Sample

Gender	N	n	%
Female	98	34	8
Male	336	118	27
Total		434	152

Description of the Instrument

The research instrument to be used in this study was a questionnaire shown in Appendix A. The questionnaire consisted of 12 questions about goals and achievement in attending college, a set of questions about attendance at the college, a set of questions about student reason for leaving, questions about degree of satisfaction with various college services, a question on plans for additional education, and demographic background questions. The purpose of this instrument was to collect data in order to establish the relation between the institutional factors and the students' attrition.

The questionnaire was submitted for the evaluation of experts in the field. Five professionals in the areas of orientation and airway sciences validated the contents of the questionnaire. The recommendations of these professionals were integrated in the instrument. The questionnaire was validated through a pilot study that was realized at a university in Puerto Rico with a different sample than the one used for these study.

The questionnaire consisted of two subscales. Subscale 1 consisted of institutional factors and subscale 2 of students attrition. Both were submitted for a statistical analysis.

Research Procedures

This section provides the guidelines used for the administration of the mailed survey using the Questionnaire to students who have dropped out.

Phase A. Preparation of Questionnaires.

The sample was drawn by computer from official institutional records and mailing labels were prepared at the same time the sample was drawn.

The initial mailing of questionnaires, cover letters, envelopes, and address labels were assembled. To track questionnaires a list was prepared in the same order as the address labels envelopes.

Phase B. Administration of questionnaires.

After the initial mailing was completed, a set of tracking sheets were prepared for recording the status of each questionnaire as it was returned. The tracking sheet contained:

1. Student's ID number.

2. Blank columns for recording the following information:

   -Date returned by post office as undeliverable.

   -Date unusable questionnaire returned or letter received; student ineligible or unable to respond.

   -Date usable questionnaire returned.

3. Blank columns for recording second mailing information:

   -Date second set of material sent.

   -Date returned by post office as undeliverable.

   -Date unusable questionnaire or letter received; student ineligible or unable to respond.

   -Date usable questionnaire returned.

Phase C. Coding of questionnaires.

1. The researcher coded each questionnaire.

2. The researcher arranged to have the data in the questionnaire processed by arranging for data entry, a computer programmer, and a computer.

3. The researcher examined and analyzed the statistical findings.

4. The researcher analyzed the research questions.

5. The researcher wrote the final report based on the findings.

Procedure for the Analysis of the Data

Questionnaires were analyzed by computing frequencies and percentages of responses for each item and by computing a cross-tabulation between certain items, where appropriate (for example: reasons for leaving by sex). The questionnaire results were conveniently divided into four categories:

-Background/status information.

-Educational goals achieved.

-Reasons for leaving.

-Evaluation of institutional services

-Current educational plans

The first step of the statistical process is a frequency distribution for each of the times that appear in the questionnaire. The number of times that each item is found and the relation between variables was tabulated by means of percentile. The following values in relation to the central tendency were considered:

a. The Mean: represents the arithmetic average.

It is computed using the following formula:

$X = x/N$

where: X = mean

x = sum of scores

N = number of cases

b. The Median: point of one distribution that leaves the same amount of cases to each side of it (Md).

c. the Mode: value of the distribution which presented with more frequency (Mo).

Cross-tabulations was presented in the computer-generated report in the order in which they appear on the questionnaire. The cross-tabulation enabled to directly compare the responses of different subgroups and to test hypotheses about some of the causal dynamics underlying particular responses.

CHAPTER IV

FINDINGS AND RESULTS

In this chapter, the findings of the analyses of the data are presented and the hypotheses of the study are tested in terms of the statistical results.

In the first section, the sample studied is described using the frequency distribution of percentages. In the second section, the hypotheses of the study are tested in terms of the statistical results by completing a cross tabulation between certain items of the questionnaire. In this section, findings results for statistically significant relationships between the variables are presented, using the Pearson product-moment correlation coefficient (Pearson r), Chi Square (X2), multiple regression (R) and analysis of variance (ANOVA). Results were considered statistically significant if alpha was equal to or less than .05 ($p<.05$).

Hypotheses

The researcher stated the following hypotheses:

H:1.0

There exists a significant relationship between satisfaction with the institutional factors and the students attrition.

H:2.0

There exists a significant relationship between the student's educational goals and decision in abandoning the Airway Science Program at Interamerican University.

H:3.0

There exists a significant relationship between the intervening variables: grade point average, the time they left the program, gender, student status, marital status and the educational goals of the students that abandoned the Airway Science Program at InterAmerican University.

Characteristics of the Sample

Number of Semesters Studied Before Dropping Out

The sample of 136 cases attended the Airway Science Program at InterAmerican University for varying numbers of semesters before dropping out. The frequency distribution for semesters attended before dropping out shows that 41.0 percent attended more than two years, 21.0 percent attended two years, 21.0 percent attended three semesters and 17.0 percent attended 2 semesters (See Figure 2).

Figure 2   Distribution for Semesters Attended Before Dropping Out

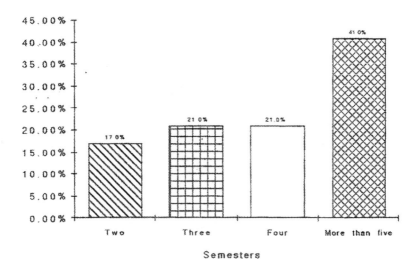

As the Figure shows, more students (41%) dropped out after more than four semesters than for any other single category. However, it can also be seen that 21 percent dropped out after three semesters. The mean time before dropping out was 4 semesters and the median was 4 semesters too. Those students who attended at least four semesters composed more than half of the sample (62 percent).

Grade Point Average Before Dropping Out

The students were asked to state the grade point average (GPA) before dropping out. Figure 3 shows the frequency distribution for GPA.

As the Figure shows, more students (37 percent) reported a GPA between 3.00 - 2.01. The percentage of students with a GPA between 4.00 - 3.01 was 21.0 percent, 26.0 percent of students have a GPA between 2.00 - 1.01. However, it may be noted that since here were 14.0 percent non-response to this item. Thus, among the respondents, only about one quarter of the dropouts had GPA's below 2.00, which contradicts the picture of the dropout as performing poorly in school.

Figure 3   Grade Point Average (GPA) Before Dropping Out

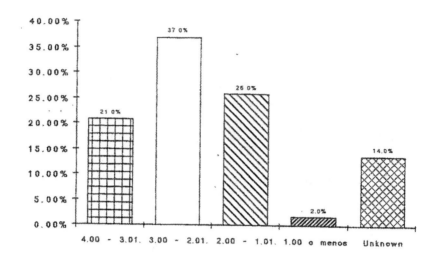

Plans to Continue Studying

The dropouts were asked to state whether they planned to continue studying in the future. The frequency distribution for the answer to this question is shown in Figure 4.

As Figure 4 shows, more than two and a half times as many of the dropouts (65 percent) said they planned to continue studying than for any single category. When those who said they intend to transfer are added to those who said "yes", nearly two thirds of the sample intend to continue studying. Only 15.0 percent said did not intend to continue studying.

Student Goals

According to the reasons that move students to drop out of InterAmerican University, they circle the letters of all of the objectives most important while they were studying at the University. In the second column, the objectives that were accomplished as a result of her or his experience at the Program.

Figura 4   Students planned to continue studying in the future

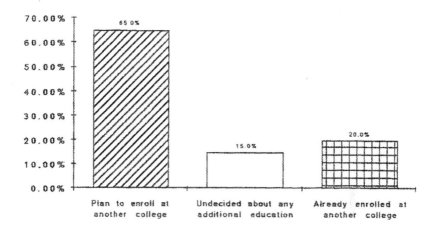

As table 2 shows, one hundred percent of the students (100%) were considered prepared for a change in work or profession in the program.

In that way it was observed that no student (0%) achieved that goal at the University. As it is observed in table 2 more than .50 percent of the students had goals as their priority. It was observed that 53.0 percent wanted to increase their knowledge, while 47 percent achieved their goal. A 94 percent desired to obtain a diploma and only a 6 percent achieved it. A 71 percent wanted to complete the necessary studies to transfer and only a 29 percent achieved it. A 100 percent wanted a change of employment or profession and noone achieved that goal. A 77 percent wanted to increase their technical knowledge, skills and/or necessary competencies for actual employment and only 23 percent achieved that goal. An 86 percent had as a goal to increase their possibilities for employment and promotion and only 14 percent achieved it. An 82 percent wanted to prepare for their first employment and only an 18 percent achieved it. A 73 percent wanted to increase their participation in cultural and social events and a 27 percent achieved it.

Table 2.   Student Goals

Goals of the University student	This goal is important to me (%)	This goal I met at Inter-American University (%)
To increase my academic knowledge.	53	47
To obtain a diploma.	94	6
Complete the necessary courses to transfer to another institution.	71	29
Prepare myself for a change of employment or profession.	100	0
Increase my knowledge, technical skills and/or competencies necessary for my actual employment.	77	23
Increase the possibilities for a promotion in my employment.	86	14
Prepare myself to obtain my first regular employment.	82	18
Increase my participation in cultural and social events.	73	27
Associate myself with other persons; make friends and meet people.	37	63
Increase my self-esteem.	65	35
Increase my skills of leadership.	73	27
Develop the ability of being independent and self suficient.	51	49

A 37 percent wanted to fraternize with others and make friendship. A 63 percent achieved that goal. A 65 percent wanted to increase his/her self esteem and a 35 percent achieved it. A 73 percent wanted to increase their skills of leadership and a 27 percent achieved it. A 51 percent wanted to develop their ability of being independent and self-sufficient. This was achieved by a 49 percent.

It is important to point out that the objective to establish interpersonal relations was achieved by more than 50 percent of the students, and almost half managed to increase their knowledge and to have the ability to be independent and self-sufficient.

Table 3 presents the percentage of students that expressed which were the most important goals for them. The most important were to increase their academic knowledge (42%), to obtain a diploma (29%) and prepare to obtain his/her first employment (9%).

The second in importance was to obtain a diploma (28%), to increase their academic knowledge (25%) and increase their knowledge or technical skills and the necessary competencies for employment (11%) (See Table 3).

Table 3   Most Important Goals to the Student

	Most important (%)	Second in importance (%)	Third in importance (%)
Increase my academic knowledge	42	25	10
Obtain a diploma	29	28	15
Complete the necessary courses to transfer to another institution	0	0	0
Prepare myself for a change of employment or profession	4	2	17
Increase my knowledge, technical skills and/or competencies necessary for my actual employment.	5	11	6
Increase the possibilities for a promotion in my employment.	2	5	0
Prepare myself to obtain my first regular employment.	9	9	10
Increase my participation in cultural and social events.	0	0	0
Associate myself with other persons; make friends and meet people.	2	2	6
Increase my self-esteem	2	4	7
Increase my skills of leadership.	0	6	10
Develop the ability of being independent and self suficient.	5	11	19

Degree Expected at InterAmerican University

According to the data collected, a 97.0 percent of the students expected to complete a bachellor's degree at InterAmerican University. Only a 3.0 percent indicated a desire for an associate degree. These data reflects the perception and ambition of the students when they arrived at the university and registered in the Program. (See Table 4).

Reasons for Dropping Out

From a list of 26 reasons for dropping out, each subject was asked to circle all the items that motivated his or her decision to drop out of the Program. Table 5, presents the reasons for dropping out.

As can be seen from Table 5, among 44 percent specified reasons stated for dropping out, money was the leading single problem. The economic factor is particularly strong when one considers that "I don't get sufficient financial aid." No percent (0%) subjects dropped out because "I believe Iam not a good student."

Table 4   Degree You Expected to Obtain at InterAmerican University

Answer	Percent (%)
I did not pursue a diploma or degree	0
Associate degree	3
Baccalaureate	97
Transfer	0

Table 5   Reasons for Dropping Out

Reasons that contributed to your decision of abandoning your studies at InterAmerican University	Percent (%)
I achieved my academic goals.	3
To transfer to another institution with more prestige than InterAmerican University	8
To transfer to another institution that offer the same specialization that I want not offered at InterAmerican University	13
I need to rest from the University.	7
The courses or programs of study that I needed were not available.	32
Not satisfied with my academic achievement.	24
Not satisfied with the quality of teaching.	29
Not satisfied with the services.	22
I am not sure of what I want to achieve.	3
I have no money to continue.	35
I did not recieve enough financial aid.	44
I achieved my personal goals.	0
I was accepted for military service.	7
I found full time employment.	15
The University is not what I expected.	13

Table 5 (cont'd)

I have much difficulty to learn.	3
I moved.	5
I could not work and go to the University at the same time.	28
Problems with my parents.	8
I believe I'm not good for studying.	0
Transporation problems.	22
I have no one to take care of my children.	0
I married.	5
Boarding problems.	5
I could not make friends.	0
Other	17

Only 3 percent dropped out because "I have difficulty in learning." Thus, the students overwhelmingly perceived themselves as being capable learners and good students, certainly not the picture of the "dump-dropout."

It is also worth noting from Table 5 that the other category indicating that 12 percent was a great category, indicating how great the number of reasons there are for why people dropout of college. The phenomenon is obviously complex and multi-faceted, making it difficult to explain with a single theory.

The Table 6 shows the most important reasons for dropping out. The economic factor is particularly strong (17%), the second specific reason was "the courses of study that I needed were not available (13%), the third reason was "I was dissatisfied with the teaching quality" (10%). It is also worth noting from Table 6 that the other category was third on the list (13%), indicating again how great the number of reasons there are for why people dropout of colleges.

Table 6   Most Important Reasons for Dropping Out

I was accepted for military service.	4	0	0
I found full time employment.	0	0	7
The University is not what I expected.	2	6	5
I have much difficulty to learn.	0	0	3
I moved.	0	2	0
I could not work and go to the University at the same time.	0	12	5
Problems with my parents.	0	0	5
I believe I'm not good for studying.	0	0	0
Transportation problems.	0	8	2
I have noone to take care of my children.	0	2	2
I married.	0	0	0
Lodging problems.	0	0	2
I could not make friends.	0	0	0
Others	13	5	12

Table 6 (cont')

From the list of reasons of the previous answer, select the three most important to you.

	Most important (%)	Second most important (%)	Third most important (%)
I achieved my academic goals.	4	0	0
To transfer to another institution with more prestige than InterAmerican University.	2	2	3
To transfer to another institution that offer the same specialization that I want not offered at InterAmerican University.	8	0	3
I need to rest from the University.	0	2	3
The courses or programs of study that I needed were not available.	13	7	12
Not satisfied with my academic achievement.	8	10	7
Not satisfied with the quality of teaching.	10	10	7
Not satisfied with the services.	4	2	10
Iam not sure of what I want to achieve.	4	0	0
I have no money to continue.	17	10	5
I did not receive enough financial aid.	9	20	7
I achieved my personal goals.	2	2	0

Satisfaction with the Services

Table 7 evaluates the satisfaction of the students with the services received from the institution. The services of the program by which the students were most satisfied were: admissions (88%), library (87%), Cafeteria (78%), bookstore (63%) and Registry (63%).

The services of InterAmerican University that demonstrated the most satisfaction to the students that abandoned the program were: Financial aid (44%), Orientation (35%), Bookstore (31%), and the Disburssment's Office (31%). The least utilized services by the students were: Audiovisual (53%), Tutoring (53%), and Student activities (45%). The services not known by the students are: services to veterans (49%), Infirmary (32%) and Program of Special Services (69%).

Hypotheses Test and Statistically Significant Relationship

Hypotheses 1.0 that predicted a significant relationship between satisfaction with the institutional factors and the students attrition was retained.

Table 7   Satisfaction with the Services

Services	I do not know this service	I know it but never used it	I used it and felt satisified	I used it but felt dissatisified
Admissions	2	4	88	6
Financial Aid	0	4	52	44
Student Activities Cultural/Sports	11	45	33	11
Services to Veterans	49	36	11	4
Library	0	2	87	11
Computer Center	8	35	33	24
Tutoring	23	53	9	15
Educational Technology Center (Audovisual)	21	53	24	2
Infirmary	32	51	11	6
Bookstore	0	6	63	31
Orientation	7	27	31	35
Disbursement Office	11	2	56	31

Registry	6	0	63	31
Federal Program of Special Services	69	18	6	7
Cafeteria		4	78	18

For its analysis a cross tabulation of variables was developed in which the level of satisfaction was correlated that the participants had with the institutional factors and the the retention of these in the Airway Science Program at InterAmerican University. The Chi square test was considered (X2), the coeficient of contingency (C) and its level of significance (p<   ) was established to .05 (p<.05). Data reflected a Chi square of 25.05 (X2=25.05) a coeficient of contingency of .31 (C=.31) with a significance level of .01 (p<.05). These data indicated that a very significant relation exist between the students satisfaction with the institutional factors and the decision to abandon the Airway Science Program at InterAmerican University of Puerto Rico. (See Table 8).

The questionnaire asked respondents to evaluate a number of services that InterAmerican University provides students. The purpose of the item was to assess student's awareness, use, and satisfaction with a particular service. To accomplish this end, each person was instructed to evaluate each service.

Table 8   Cross Tabulation by the relationship between the satisfaction with the Institutional Factors and the Attrition

Variables	Chi square	Contingency coefficient	Significance Level
Attrition and Satisfaction with Institutional Factors	25.05	.31	.01**

** Significance to level .01 (p<.01)

In one of four ways each person evaluate the service: (1) I did not know about this service, (2) I knew about this service but did not use it, (3) I used this service and was satisfied with it, and (4) I used this service but was not satisfied with it.

Table 7 presents the services each respondent was asked to evaluate and identifies the number of percentage of responding selecting each of the four response options. It should be noted that while Federal Program of Special Services was listed as one of the InterAmerican University services to be evaluated, the college does not have any formally recognized service in this area.

The five services that respondents indicated are most satisfactory and least satisfactory. The ranking of services was determined by calculating the proportion of students using the service who were satisfied with it (number of students who used the service and were satisfied with it (divided by the total of students who used the service). As the data show in Table 7, the InterAmerican University admission office ranked as the most satisfactory service in terms of the proportion of students who used it.

In interpreting the services that ranked least satisfactory, a low proportion of the persons who usedf the financial aid office evaluated it as satisfactory. This is cause for some concern. Academic advising (counseling) and the disbursement office are critical to ensure effective student planning and performance.

The dependent variable in the study, the number of semesters the student attended the Airway Science Program at InterAmerican University before dropping out, was correlated with the interval scale independent variables in the study. For the variables involving evaluation of University services, the students who used and were satisfied with each of the following services stayed the most semesters, on average, before dropping out: (a) admissions (mean = 3.45), (b) the library (mean = 3.55), (c) cafeteria (mean = 3.56) and (d) registrar's office (mean = 3.66) (See Table 9).

For the following University services, the student who used and disagreed (were not satisfied) with the services stayed the most semesters, on average before dropping out: (a) Financial aid office (mean = 4.29), (b) counseling (mean 3.91), (c) the bookstore (mean = 3.78) and (d) disbursement office (mean = 4.50) (See Table 9).

Table 9   Level of satisfaction by semesters average with the university services

Service	Satisfied $\overline{X}$	Not Satisfied $\overline{X}$
Admissions	3.45	
Library	3.55	
Cafeteria	3.56	
Registrar's Office	3.66	
Financial Aid Office		4.29
Counseling		3.91
Bookstore		3.78
Disbursement Office		4.50

Many of the independent variables in the study were nominal scales with more than two categories. To assess the relationship between these variables and the interval scale dependent variable (number of semesters enrolled before dropping out), analysis of Variance (ANOVA), was employed. The following relationships were found to be statistically significant; shown in Table 10.

These findings indicated that significant statistical differences exist between the evaluation of the variables or institutional factors and the number of semesters that the student was enrolled. It was observed that those students that decided to abandon the Airway Science Program by being disatisfied with the institutional services had more than three or four semesters in the Airway Science Program (See Table 10).

Hypotheses 2.0 that predicted a significant relationship between the students' goals and decision in abandoning the Airway Science Program at InterAmerican University was retained. For this analysis the number of reasons that motivated the students decisions to dropout, and the students educational goals, a correlation and regression analysis was used with test of significance for the calculated r value.

Table 10   Analysis of vaiance (ANOVA)

Variable	Between groups mean square	Within groups mean square	F - ratio
Degree expectation	12.91	6.82	1.89 *
How do you evaluate the cafeteria?	6.82	2.33	2.93 *
How do you evaluate transportation to Bayamon Campus?	9.86	2.17	4.54 **
How do you evaluate the Registrar's Office?	7.95	2.22	3.58 *
How do you evaluate the disbursement Office?	10.58	2.13	4.96 **

* Significance at .05 level p < .5
** Significance at .01 level p < .1

The test of significance was established at .05 (p<.05). When a step-wise regression was employed, the two variables that were statistically related to the reasons for abandoning the college were the economic factor and dissatisfaction with the Program. (r=.32) (p<.01) (See Table 11). As table 2 shows, the goal pursued by the largest majority of all respondents was "to prepare myself for a change of employment or profession (100 percent). This second most pursued goal (94 percent) was to obtain a bachellor's degree. Corresponding, these two goals ranked the highest as goals achieved by the total respondents group.

As Table 2 shows, the most important goal by the largest majority of all respondents was "to increase my knowledge and understanding in an academic field" (42 percent). The second most pursued goal (29 percent was to obtain a bachellor's degree. According to this responses, this group was specially interested in (1) increasing their knowledge and understanding in an academic field, (2) obtaining a bachellor degree, (3) preparing for a new career and (4) preparing to obtain a regular employment.

Table 11 Relationship between the students goals and the reasons that motivated the decisions to dropout

Variables	(%) Mean X	Standard Deviation SD	Regression Coefficient r	Significance Level $p < \alpha$
Prepare for employment or profession	100.0	5.0		
and				
Economic factor	56.00	3.4	.32	.01 **
Dissatisfaction with the Program	58.00	6.0		

** Significance at level .01 <

The questionnaire provided data from which students' reasons for leaving were tabulated. Table 6 summarizes the response of the group with respect to this item. The table shows the two most important reasons for students' leaving. While no single pattern emerges from Table 6 across the group or across the two top-ranked reasons, several points are noteworthy:

-Lack of money and inability to earn enough money deter program completion.

-Dissatisfaction with the learning environment.

Hypothesis 3.0 that predicts a significant relationship between the intervening variables, grade point average, gender, students status, marital status and the educational goals of the students that abandoned the Airway Science Program at InterAmerican University was retained. For this analysis a crosstabulation was the computer generate report were developed. The cross tabulation compared the responses of the students. The most important goals is: increase knowledge. A chi square test shows 24.56 ($X2=24.56$), with a contingency coefficient of .43 ($C=.43$) and a level of significance less of .01 ($p<.01$).

The second goal was to obtain a bachellor's degree. A Chi Square test shows 63.43 (X2=63.43), with a contingency coefficient was .57 (C=57) and a significance level of .01 (p<.01). The third most important goal was to prepare for their first job. The Chi square was 54.16 (X2=54.16), the contingency coefficient was .45(C=.45) with a significance level of .01 (p<.01). With this findings, hypotheses 3.0 was retained. There is a significant statistically relationship between the Grade Point Average (GPA) on the moment that they abandoned the Program and the educational goal of the students that abandoned the Airway Science Program at InterAmerican University. (See Table 12).

The crosstabulation with the relationship between the most important goals and the gender shows the following findings: a Chi square equal to 5.01 (X = 5.01), a contingency coefficient of .10 (C= .10) at a significance level of .24 (p >.05) for the goal of increase knowledge; for the goal of obtain a bachellor degree the Chi square was 4.07 (X = 4.07), a contingency coefficient of .09 (C=.09) at a significance level of .26 (p>.05); and for the goal to prepare for their first job the Chi square was 2.54 (x =2.54).

Table 12 Relationship between the most important educational goals and the grade point average (G.P.A.)

Variables	CHI Square (X^2)	Contingency Coefficient (C)	Level of Significance $(p < \alpha)$
Grade Point Average (GPA)			
and			
Most important goals:			
Increase Knowledge	24.56	.43	.001**
Obtain a degree	63.43	.57	.001**
Prepare for their first job	54.16	.45	.01**

** Significance at level .01 (p < .01)

The contingency coefficient was .03 (C=.03) at a significance level of .45 (p>.05). There is not a significant statistically relationship between the gender and the educational goals of the students that abandoned the Airway Science Program at Interamerican University (See Table 13).

The crosstabulation with the relationship between the student status and the most important goals shows the following findings: a Chi square test of 2.54 (X =2.54) for the goal of increase knowledge, a contingency coefficient of .24 (C=.24) at a significance level of .46 (p>.05); for the goal of obtain a bachellor degree the Chi square was 1.58 (X =1.58), a contingency coefficient of .15 (C=.15) at a significance level of .42 (p>.05); for the goal to prepare for the first job the Chi square was 1.32 (X =1.32), a contingency coefficient of .11 (C=.11) at a significance level of .63 (p>.05). There is not a significant statiscally relationship between the student status and the educational goals of the students that abandoned the Airway Science Program at Interamerican University (See Table 14).

Table 13 Relationship between the most important goals and the gender

Variables	CHI Square (X^2)	Contingency Coefficient (C)	Level of Significance $(p < \infty)$
Gender			
and			
Most important goals:			
Increase Knowledge	5.01	.10	.24 N.S.
Obtain a degree	4.07	.09	.26 N.S.
Prepare for their			
first job	2.54	.03	.45 N.S.

N.S. Significant (p > .05)

Table 14 Relationship between the most important educational goals and the student status

Variables	CHI Square (X^2)	Contingency Coefficient (C)	Level of Significance $(p < \infty)$
Student Status			
and			

Most important goals:			
Increase Knowledge	2.54	.24	.46 N.S.
Obtain a degree	1.58	.15	.42 N.S.
Prepare for their			
first job	1.32	.11	.63 N.S.

N.S. Significant (p > .05)

The crosstabulation with the relationship between the marital status and the most important goals shows the followings findings: a Chi square test of 1.68 (X =1.68) for the goal of increase knowledge, a contingency coefficient of .05 (C=.05) at a significance level of .49 (p>.05); for the goal of obtain a bachellor's degree the Chi square was .39 (C=.39), a contingency coefficient of .03 (C=.03) at a significance level of .65 (p>.05); for the goal to preepare for the first job the Chi square was 2.32 (X =2.32), a contingency coefficient of .09 (C=.09) at a significance level of .49 (p>.05). There is not a significant statiscally relationship between the marital status of the students and the educational goals. (See Table 15).

Summary

In sum, the numbers of semesters students were in the Airway Science Program at InterAmerican University before dropping out was related to their grade point average, the degree they expected to receive, the number of services they used and found satisfactory.

Table 15 Relationskp between the most important educational goals and the marital status

Variables	CHI Square (X^2)	Contingency Coefficient (C)	Level of Significance $(p < \infty)$
Marital Status			
and			

Most important goals:			
Increase Knowledge	1.68	.05	.49 N.S.
Obtain a degree	.39	.03	.65 N.S.
Prepare for their			
first job	2.32	.09	.46 N.S.

N.S. Significant ($p > .05$)

And also, with their type of satisfaction (satisfied or not satisfied) with 12 university services: cafeteria, registrar's office, the disbursement office, counseling, the bookstore, the infirmary, the audiovisual center, the computer center, the library, admissions, and student activities/cultural/sports.

More of the students before dropping out reported a GPA between 3.00 - 2.01 and dropped out after more than four semesters than for any other single period of time.

Among the group, three reasons for leaving the Program surfaced an important conflict between job and studies, and lack of money. The students frequently mentioned dissatisfaction with the learning environment.

CHAPTER V

CONCLUSIONS, IMPLICATIONS, AND RECOMMENDATIONS

This study was conducted to determine the factors associated with student attrition at the Airway Science Program at InterAmerican University of Puerto Rico. This chapter includes the conclusions, implications and recommendations.

Conclusions

Based on the analysis of data collected we arrived at the following conclusions:

1. There is significant relationship between the satisfaction with the university services and the number of semesters that students attended the Airway Science Program at Interamerican University before dropping out.

2. There are significant differences between the evaluation of institutional factors and the number of semesters that the students were enrolled.

3. There is a significant relationship between the students goals and the decision in abandoning the Airway Science Program at Interamerican University.

4. There is a significant relationship between the grade point average and the educational goals of the students that abandoned the Airway Science Program at Interamerican University.

5. There is not a significant relationship between the gender, students' status and marital status and the educational goals of the students that abandoned the Airway Science Program at Interamerican University.

6. The single common specific reason given was a lack of money to continue studies.

7. The educational factor reason the student gave for dropping out was: "the courses I need were not available".

8. Dissatisfaction with University services ranked relatively very low.

9. The great majority of the students in the study stated that they were capable learners rather than slow learners.

10. The highest percentage of students who dropped out had a high grade point average.

11. The number of semesters that the students attended the Program before dropping out were correlated with the Grade, point, average.

12. The more services the students used and found satisfactory, the more semesters they should have stayed

at the Airway Science Program at the InterAmerican University.

13. The satisfaction indicated a positive experience at the InterAmerican University, and thus have delayed a prevented drop out behavior.

14. The less satisfied the students were with the services at the Program, the fewer semesters they stayed at the University before dropping out.

Implications

Hypotheses 1.0 that predicted a significant relationship between satisfaction with the institutional factors and students attrition was retained. The findings reflect that there is a significant relationship between satisfaction with the university services and the number of semesters that students attended the Airway Science Program. There are significant differences between the evaluation of institutional factors and the number of semesters that the student was enrolled. The major dependent variable examined in the study was the number of semesters students were enrolled in the Airway Science Program before they dropped out. The primary idea behind using this variable was that the longer the students stayed at the University, the more satisfied it is presumed they were with the curriculum and services, and conversely, the fewer semesters they stayed, the less satisfied they were presumed to have been with the curriculum and services. However, it is also known that other factors could have played a significant part in affecting the decisions of the students to dropout of the university, e.g., their grade point average, which measures the degree to which they were successful in their academic studies.

As will be recalled from the previous chapter, the study found that more students dropped out after four semesters than for any other single amount of time. This would seem to indicate that more of the dropouts were satisfied with conditions at the University than were quickly dissatisfied with them. This pattern seem to indicate that students decisions to dropout was not and easy one; that these students were intending to complete their course of studies before dropping out.

The literature in the field of student attrition suggested that there are a multitude of reasons for students dropping out of college before graduation. No studies the researcher could find, however, examined the phenomenon of student attrition at Airway Science Program at InterAmerican University. The researcher, therefore, undertook a study to fill this gap in the literature while, at the same time, exploring a wide variety of variables considered to be related to student attrition.

Hypotheses 2.0 that predicted a significant relationship between the students' educational goals and decision in abandoning the Airway Science Program was retained. The findings reflect that there is a significant relationship between the students' goals and the decision in abandoning the Airway Science Program at Interamerican University. The findings suggest that dropping out may, therefore, only be a temporary phenomenon among students at InterAmerican University, rather than indicate the end of the students' formal educational careers. The findings could indicate, for example, that temporary circumstances motivated the students to discontinue their studies, and that circumstances could involve their personal lives, conditions at the University, or both of these factors.

In the study, the subjects were asked to state the reasons they dropped out at the University, and it was clearly shown that the single common specific reason given was a lack of money to continue their studies. This was evidenced by two statements: "I don't have money to continue studies" and, "I don't get sufficient financial aid". These were the two most commonly given specific reasons involved and educational factors the students wanted to transfer to get the specialization they wanted. This would indicate that they were mistaken in picking InterAmerican University as the college appropriate for them. It would seem plausible to speculate, from their answer, that they only learned about the possible inappropriateness of Airway Science Program for them after they started their course of study at the University. This reasoning would seem to be supported by another relatively common reason the student gave for dropping out: "The courses I needed were not available".

It is also interesting to note that, from among the list of reasons the students gave for dropping out, dissatisfaction with University services ranked relatively very low. The great majority of the students in the study stated that they thought they were capable learners rather than slow learners or lacking the intelligence necessary to handle the curriculum at the University.

Hypotheses 3.0 that predicted a significant relationship between the intervening variables and the educational goals of the students that abandoned the Airway Science Program at InterAmerican University was retained. The findings reflect that there is a significant relationship between the grade point average and the educational goals of the students that abandoned the Airway Science Program. There is not a significant relationship between the gender, students' status and marital status and the educational goals of the students that abandoned the Airway Science Program.

When it comes to the relationship between dropping out and grade point average, this study found a result which contradicts the common picture of the dropout as the poorest academic performer. In the results section, it was noted that only 2.0 percent of those who dropped out had a grade point average of 1.0 or less. On the other hand, the highest percentage of students who dropped out (58.0%) had a grade point average of between 4.00 - 2.01. Why might it be that those students with the highest grade point average were also the ones who were most likely to dropout?

Clearly, this is a subject that requires further research. If it is true that merely having a high grade point average does not act as a buffer against student attrition, then administrative programs aimed at combating student attrition solely through increases of services may be futile attempts at preventing students from dropping out.

When the number of semesters the students attend the Program before dropping out were correlated with the other variables in the study, it was found that only a few of the factors examined emerged as statistically significant. One such correlation involved the student grade point average and the number of semesters they attended the University before dropping out. For this relationship, the Pearson r=.32

(p<.01), showed a positive relationship. This means that, generally speaking, the higher the students' grade point average, the more semesters they stayed at InterAmerican University before dropping out. However, it should be noted that r=.31 is a modest relationship, which shows that there were many exceptions to this pattern; that is, students who had a lower grade point average also stayed at the University a greater number of semesters than might have expected from their low academic performance.

A major intent of the study was to analyze the relationship between the number of University services the student uses and found satisfactory, and the number of semesters they stayed in school before dropping out. The idea behind this was that the more services the students used and found satisfactory, the more semesters they should have stayed at the Airway Science Program at InterAmerican University. This is because such satisfaction would seem to have indicated a positive experience at the University, and thus have delayed or prevented drop out behavior. For this relationship between the number of services the student used and found satisfactory and the number of semesters they attended the University before dropping out, the Pearson r was, in fact, r=.32 (p<.01).

This result confirms the general expectation of increased satisfaction being associated with longevity at the Program. Conversely, it means that the less satisfied the students were with the services at the University, the fewer semesters they stayed at the University before dropping out.

This study of the factors related to student attrition at the Airway Science Program at InterAmerican University identified several independent variables that were significantly related to the number of semesters the students attended the University before dropping out.

As with other studies in the field, discussed in the Review of the Literature, this study confirmed the student attrition is a highly complex phenomenon, apparently determined by multiple variables interacting simultaneouly.

Recommendations

In light of the conclusions and implications of this study, the following recommendations are presented:

1. The institution should develop an awareness of the needs of students with a high G.P.A. have in order to secure their retention.

2. A plan of action which focuses on all personal and institutional factors that affect student retention and fosters their achievement of educational goals should be designed.

3. The services listed below, in the order of precedence, should be improved for the Airway Science Program students at InterAmerican University.

   a) Federal program of special services.
   b) Services to veterans.
   c) Financial aid.
   d) Availability of most needed courses.
   e) Quality of teaching.
   f) Infirmary.
   g) Tutoring.
   h) Educational technical center (Audiovisuals).
   i) Availability of transportation to aeronautical facilities.

4. As far as career planning is concerned, additional analysis needs to be conducted to determine the extent to which students who desire a particular service are getting it.

5. Follow-up studies should be done with the purpose of validating the institutional factors that affect student retention in the Airway Science Program at InterAmerican University.

6. Comparative studies with other institutional programs should be developed in order to determine the factors that affect student retention.

BIBLIOGRAPHY

Airhart, P. M. (1987) Prediction and follow up of community college droputs and persister. (Doctoral Dissertation, Texas Woman's University, 1987). Dissertation Abstracts International. 48/10A.

Attrition '89 (1989). Attrition '89: A survey of non-returning students in spring 1989. Research report 89-04. Vineland, NJ: Cumberland County College. (ERIC Document Reproduction Service No. ED 308 887).

Brophy, D. A. (1986). Follow-up study of the fall 1984 Sierra College dropouts. Rocklin, CA: Sierra Joint Community College District. (ERIC Document Reproduction Service No. ED 277 420).

Bross, T. M. (1985). Social network, social support and persistence in GED programs. (Doctoral Dissertation, Rutgers The State University of New Jersey, New Brunswick, 1985). Dissertation Abstracts International, 46/09A.

Carroll, J. (1988). Freshman retention and attrition factors at a predominantly black urban community college. Journal of College Student Development, 29 (1), 52-59.

Carrol, J. (1988). Factors affecting academic success and dropout bahavior among black freshmen students at a predominantly black urban community college.(Doctoral Dissertation, Columbia University Teachers College, 1986). Dissertation Abstracts International, 47/06A.

Carter, G. F. (1986). Factors related to college attrition; A validation of the Tinto model withdrawal at three class levels. (Doctoral Dissertation, The University of Michigan, 1986). Dissertation Abstracts International, 47/10A.

Giddan, N. S., Levy, D. M., Estroff, R. M., & Cline, J. C. (1987). College counseling and student retention: Data and speculations. Journal of College Students Psychotherapy, 1 (3), 5-28.

Gille, S. V. (1985). The influence of social and academic integration and use of campus services on freshman attrition. (Doctoral Dissertation, University of Missouri, Kansas City, 1985). Dissertation Abstracts International, 47/01A.

Gittens, E. R. (1987). Student perceptions of the effects of the cooperative education curriculum at Fiorello H. LaGuardia community college. (Doctoral Dissertation, Fordham University, 1987). Dissertation Abstracts International, 47/098.

Glennen, R. E., Baxley, D. M., & Farren, P. J. (1985). Impact of intrusive advising on minority student retention. College Student Journal, 19(4), 335-338.

Gosman, E. et al. (1983). Predicting student progression: The influence of race and other student and institutional characteristics on college student performance. Research in Higher Education, 18, 209-237.

Hellmich, D. M. (1989). Students retention within targeted english courses at Santa Fe Community College. Santa Fe, FL: University of Florida. (ERIC Document Reproduction Service No. ED 308-908).

Kaliszeski, M. S. (1986). Clark's "cooling out" concept as a factor in student completion of communitgy college programs. Dissertation Abstracts Interanational, 47/11A.

Koehler, L. (1984). What's tutoring worth? A report on retention and cost effectiveness. Cincinnati, OH: University of Cincinnati. (ERIC Document Reproduction Service No. ED 296-689).

Kowalski, C. J. (1982). College dropouts: Some research findings. Psychology A Quarterly Journal of Human Behavior, 19 (2-3), 45-49.

Leblanc, D. S. (1986). A descriptive assessment of dropout/stopout patterns in California community colleges as perceived by counselors (Doctoral Dissertation, University of La Verne, 1986). Dissertation Abstracts International, 47/07A.

Lee, R. E. (1988). Assessing retention program holding power effectiveness across smaller community colleges. Journal of Colleges Students Development, 29 (3), 255-262.

Mallinckrodt, B. (1988). Student retention, social support, and dropout intention: Comparison of black and white students. Jounal of College Student Development, 29 (1), 60-64.

Marinaccio, J. (1985). Attrition at community colleges. Princeton, N.J: Princeton University. (ERIC Document Reproduction Service No. ED 265-908).

McClain, R. S. & Sartwell, D. (1983). A study of freshman student withdrawal at Salem State College. Salem, Mass: Salem State College. (ERIC Document Reproduction Service No. ED 234 674).

Meznek, J. (1989). The Puente Project. Sacramento, CA: California Community Colleges. (ERIC Document Reproduction Service No. ED 307 920).

Middleton, E. E. (1987). Opinions of black persisters and dropouts concerning selected environmental factors at Ohio University. (Doctoral Dissertation, Ohio University, 1987). Dissertation Abstracts International, 48/04A.

Nelson, R. B., & Urff, D. M. (1982). Withdrawing/nonreturning students at the University of North Dakota. Grand Forks, ND: University of North Dakota. (ERIC Document Reproduction Service No. ED 221 098).

Nettles, M. T., Thoeny, A. R., & Gosman, E. J. (1986). Comparative and predictive analysis of black and white students' college achievement and experiences. Journal of Higher Education, 57 (3), 289-318.

Nettles, M. T., & Johnson, J. R. (1987). Raca, sex, and other factors as determinants of college students' socialization. Special issue: Blacks in U.S. higher education. Journal of College Student Personnel, 28 (6), 512-524.

Olagunju, A. O. (1981). Direct assessment and treatment of attrition and retention problems. Concord, NC: Barber-Scotia College. (ERIC Document Reproduction Service No. ED 224 370).

Robinson, L. F. (1989). The effect of freshman transition to college/ orientation courses on student retention. College Student Journal, 23 (3), 225-229.

Rysberg, J. A. (1986). Effects of modifying instruction in a college classroom. Psychological Reports, 58 (3), 965-966.

Spaights, E., Dixon, H. E. & Nickolai, S. (1985). Racism in higher education. College Student Journal, 19 (1), 17-22.

Tambe, J. T. (1984). Predicting persistence and withdrawal of open admissions students at Virginia State University. Journal of Negro Education, 53 (4), 406-417.

Todd, J. U. (1986). The relationship between student retention and financial aid at a large urban community college: A case study. (Doctoral Dissertation, The University of Texas at Austin, 1986). Dissertation Abstracts International, 47/12A.

Trippi, J. F., & Baker, S. B. (1989). Student and residential correlates of black student grade performance and persistence at a predominantly white university campus. Journal of College Student Development, 30 (2), 136-143.

VonDestinon, M. (1988). Chicano student persistence: The effects of integration and involvement. Internal report series, report No. 14. Tucson, AZ: Arizona University. (ERIC Document Reproduction Service No. ED 299 939).

Walter, G. G. (1987). Attrition and accommodation of hearing-impaired college students in the US. Rochester, NY: Rochester Institute of Technology, NY. National Technical Institute for the Deaf. ERIC Document Repoduction Service No. ED 304 856).

White, W. F., & Shahan, J. M. (1989). College student motivation and retention system. College Student Journal, 23 (3), 230-233.

Wilder, J. R. (1983). Retention in higher education. Psychology A Quarterly Journal of Human Behavior, 20 (2), 4-9.

Williamson, D. R. (1986). Dropouts from community colleges: Path analysis of a national sample. (Doctoral Dissertation, Virginia Polytechnic Institute and State University, 1986). Dissertation Abstracts International, 47/07A.

Dear student:

The attached questionnaire concerned with student desertion from the Airway Science Program is part of a study being carried on by the Airway Science Program at Interamerican University of Puerto Rico. This project is concerned specifically with determining the factors involved with student desertion from the Airway Science Program. The results of this study will help to provide preliminary criteria to be used for developing better selection procedures and for improving the Airway Science training program at Interamerican University.

We are particularly desirous of obtaining your responses because it will contribute significantly toward solving some of the problems we face in this important area of education. The enclosed questionaire has been tested with a sample of 250 students from another institution. The average time required to answer the questionnaire was 10 minutes.

It will be appreciated if you will complete the questionnaire prior to November 1 and return it in the stamped envelope enclosed. Other phases of this research cannot be carried out until we have a complete analysis of the questionnaire data. We would welcome any comments that you may have concerning any aspect of principal selection not covered in the questionnaire. I will be pleased to send you a summary of questionnaire results if you desire. Thank you for your cooperation.

Sincerely,

Rafael Alverio, Jr.
Project Director
Airway Science Program

APPENDIX A
QUESTIONNAIRE

UNIVERSIDAD INTERAMERICANA

Estimado exalumno:

La Universidad Interamericana, en su empeño por identificar las causas que motivan a sus estudiantes a abandonar su estadía en la institución, decidió desarrollar un estudio. Necesitamos toda tu cooperación para determinar exactamente las razones que te llevaron a cambiar tu decisión de permanecer en nuestra institución.

Deseamos que contestes el cuestionario que se incluye a la mayor brevedad posible y lo devuelvas utilizando el sobre predirigido.

1. Las siguientes premisas reflejan las metas de muchos estudiantes universitarios. En la primera columna circula las letras de aquellas metas importantes para ti cuando estabas matriculado en nuestra universidad. En la segunda columna circula las letras de las metas que tú consideras que lograste como resultado de las experiencias en nuestra institución.

    Esta meta es importante para mí.

    Esta meta la logré en la Universidad Interamericana.

A	A	Aumentar mis conocimientos académicos.
B	B	Obtener un diploma.
C	C	Completar los cursos necesarios para transferirme a otra institución.
D	D	Prepararme para un cambio de empleo o profesión.
E	E	Aumentar mis conocimientos, destrezas técnicas y/o competencias necesarias para mi empleo actual.
F	F	Aumentar las posibilidades de un ascenso en mi empleo.
G	G	Prepararme para obtener mi primer empleo regular.
H	H	Aumentar mi participación en eventos culturales y sociales.
I	I	Relacionarme con otras personas; hacer amistades y conocer gente.
J	J	Aumentar mi autoestima.
K	K	Aumentar mis destrezas de liderato.
L	L	Desarrollar la habilidad de ser independiente y autosuficiente.

2. De la lista de metas de la pregunta anterior, selecciona las tres más importantes para ti.

    _____ Más importante
    _____ Segunda en importancia
    _____ Tercera en importancia

3. ¿Qué grado esperabas obtener en la Universidad Interamericana?

    _____ No buscaba un diploma o grado.
    _____ Grado Asociado.
    _____ Bachillerato.
    _____ Traslado

4. La decisión de abandonar una institución universitaria puede estar motivada por una variedad de razones. Por favor, circula las letras de todas las razones que contribuyeron a tu decisión de abandonar tus estudios en la Universidad Interamericana.

A   Logré mis metas académicas.
B   Para transferirme a otra institución que tenga más prestigio que la Universidad Interamericana.
C   Para transferirme a otra institución que ofrezca la especialidad que yo quiero y que la Universidad Interamericana no ofrece.
D   Necesito descansar de la universidad.
E   Los cursos o programas de estudios que necesitaba no estaban disponibles.
F   Insatisfacción con mi aprovechamiento académico.
G   Insatisfacción con la calidad de la enseñanza.
H   Insatisfacción con los servicios.
I   No estoy seguro de lo que quiero lograr.
J   No tengo dinero para continuar.
K   No obtuve suficiente ayuda económica.
L   Logré mis metas personales.
M   Me aceptaron para el servicio militar.
N   Conseguí empleo a tiempo completo.
O   La universidad no era lo que yo esperaba.
P   Tengo mucha dificultad para aprender.
Q   Me mudé.
R   No pude trabajar e ir a la universidad al mismo tiempo.
S   Problemas con mis padres.
T   Creo que no sirvo para estudiar.
U   Problemas de transportación.
V   No tengo quien me cuide mis hijos.
W   Me casé.
X   Problemas de hospedaje.
Y   No pude hacer amistades.
Z   Otros _____

5. De la lista de razones de la pregunta anterior, selecciona las tres más importantes para ti.

____ Más importante
____ Segunda en importancia
____ Tercera en importancia

6. ¿Cuánto tiempo estuviste matriculado en nuestra universidad?

____ Un semestre
____ Un año (2 semestres)
____ Un año y medio (3 semestres)
____ Dos años (4 semestres)
____ Más de 2 años

7. De las siguientes, ¿cuál era tu área de estudio?

____ Administración de Empresas (Gerencia, Contabilidad, etc.)
____ Artes y Ciencias
____ Ciencias Secretariales
____ Educación y Tecnología

8. ¿Cuál era tu promedio académico cuando decidiste abandonar la Universidad Interamericana?

___ 4.00 - 3.01
___ 3.00 - 2.01
___ 2.00 - 1.01
___ 1.00 o menos
___ Dezconozco

9. ¿Eras estudiante ...

___ a tiempo completo?
___ a tiempo parcial?
___ nocturno?
___ sabatino?

10. Los siguientes servicios son provistos por las universidades. ¿Cómo evalúas estos servicios en nuestra institución?

No conozco este servicio.

   Lo conozco pero nunca lo utilicé.

      Lo utilicé y me sentí satisfecho con él.

         Utilicé el servicio pero me sentí insatisfecho con él.

A	B	C	D	Admisiones
A	B	C	D	Asistencia Económica
A	B	C	D	Actividades Estudiantiles/ Culturales/ Deportivas
A	B	C	D	Servicios a Veteranos
A	B	C	D	Biblioteca
A	B	C	D	Centro de Cómputos
A	B	C	D	Tutorías
A	B	C	D	Centro Tecnología Educativa (Audiovisual)
A	B	C	D	Enfermería
A	B	C	D	Librería
A	B	C	D	Orientación
A	B	C	D	Pagaduría
A	B	C	D	Programa de Cooperación Educativa
A	B	C	D	Registraduría
A	B	C	D	Programa Federal de Servicios Especiales
A	B	C	D	Transportación
A	B	C	D	Cafetería

11. ¿Estás casado actualmente?

___ Sí ___ No

12. ¿Tienes planes de continuar estudiando?

___ No
___ Sí
___ No estoy decidido
___ Me fui a otra institución